*This is for Oliver, Charlotte, Nathalia,
Cameron, Rory, Erin, Holly and Heston.*

In August 2006, Poohka, the main character of this story, was living as a feral cat on a private estate in Sotogrande, southern Spain. Poohka went missing for over a month and, when he eventually returned on the 23rd September, he had a very badly broken leg. To this day, no one knows how the injury happened or where he was during this traumatic time in his life.

Only Poohka knows and this is his amazing story!

I would like to believe it is true (albeit a little far-fetched!).

Contents

Chapter 1 - A bad day to be hungry

Sotogrande, Andalucía, southern Spain.

Life in Sotogrande was good for Poohka and his friends. He enjoyed the freedom of living on a private estate, he was fed a healthy meal once a day, and he had a good circle of friends. What more could he possibly want?

'Morning, 3jabs,' Poohka called to his best friend. 'Did you have a good night's hunting?'

'Mate, it was brilliant,' 3jabs replied as he groomed his rather grubby-looking coat. Poohka liked that 3jabs was more intent on enjoying himself than wasting precious time on his appearance. Life was too short, so 3jabs lived life to the full. No exceptions!

'3jabs, will you tell me the story of how you got your name?' Poohka asked.

'What, again?' said 3jabs. But Poohka knew that 3jabs loved telling the tale. The highlight of his day was explaining to any new cats passing through, especially the young ladies, how he had actually got his name. And Poohka never tired of hearing it – he was so very proud of his loyal friend.

'Well, you see, it happened like this,' 3jabs recalled. 'I was waiting patiently for my daily meal to arrive, close to the workers' hut, when – blow me down – I smelt the most delicious aroma of sardines coming from a newly deposited large wooden box. You know me, I'm an easy target when it comes to my food, and I could not resist the temptation.'

3jabs took a deep breath, paused briefly, then continued. 'So I cautiously made my way over to the box. The smells were so overpowering by this stage, but I was aware of Greta, the tall elegant lady who took it in turns to feed us, standing close by, so I told myself to be on my guard...'

Dribble had started dripping from 3jabs's mouth as he swapped his story for a daydream. Poohka coughed.

'Where was I?' he exclaimed, licking his lips. 'Yes, well, to cut a long story short, I succumbed – I walked straight into the box. Bingo – the door to the box slammed shut!' 3jabs jumped on all fours as he spoke. 'I had walked into a trap!'

'What happened next?' Poohka asked, his attention fixed on his best friend.

'I was not going to give up easily, so I hissed and I clawed the wire frame at the other end of the wooden box, then, of course, I hissed some more.' 3jabs chuckled. 'But all the while, the sardines were practically talking to me, telling me to eat their fishy delights. So I quietened down and devoured them with so much relish, I nearly forgot I was trapped inside the wooden cage. The next thing I knew, I was being picked up in the box. Then I heard a car door slam, and an engine start. I do not understand why humans want to get into those fast-moving vehicles; I cannot see the point of them,' 3jabs grumbled. 'Anyway, after a terrible journey – no creature like myself has ever experienced so many pot holes in such a ramshackle road – eventually we arrived at a building that made my stomach turn,' 3jabs said. 'I'm not boring you, am I?'

'Oh no, not at all,' said Tigs, who was sitting closest to 3jabs, to the right of Poohka. Tigs had heard the story many times too, but all the young cats enjoyed the tale.

'Well, as I was saying, we entered this white, clinical-looking building and were met by the owner of the joint: Antonio. He's not a man I ever want to see again! My senses told me to be very cautious of him. "What have we here?" Antonio asked in perfect

English. "Oh, just another cat from our estate to be neutered," replied Greta. "Can I leave him with you, and we will collect him tomorrow?" "Of course, any time after twelve tomorrow will be fine," said Antonio.'

3jabs turned his head slowly to all the cats in his audience. '"Just another cat" she said! And of course I am not 'just another cat' – so I had to prove they were wrong. The wooden box was carried into a yellow painted room with white tables and metal instruments everywhere. I was placed on the table in the centre of the room and the young assistant came across, gave me gooey eyes and chatted to me through the wire netting. Meanwhile, the door at the other end was being slowly opened by Antonio the vet. What the idiots did not realize was I could see everything going on in the mirror hanging on the wall behind the assistant!

"Keep the cat's attention, Anya," said Antonio, "while I give him a quick injection to put him out."

"Put me out" he said! Well, no one is ever going to put ME out.' 3jabs gave a hiss into the air, then looked down again to check that Poohka, Tigs and the others were still paying attention.

'I turned round so swiftly that I just caught the tip of the syringe in my shoulder. I winced with pain but wasn't going to stop now. Then Antonio withdrew his hand, giving me the perfect opportunity to escape,' 3jabs went on. 'I was feeling a little woozy, but I still had all my marbles. Then I saw that the door to the room was closed, and so were the windows. My chances were slim but I could not give up now. If I could just jump at the door handle, I could escape this room and the terrible syringe. I darted one way, the assistant close on my tail, during which time Antonio was setting up another syringe to plant into my backside.

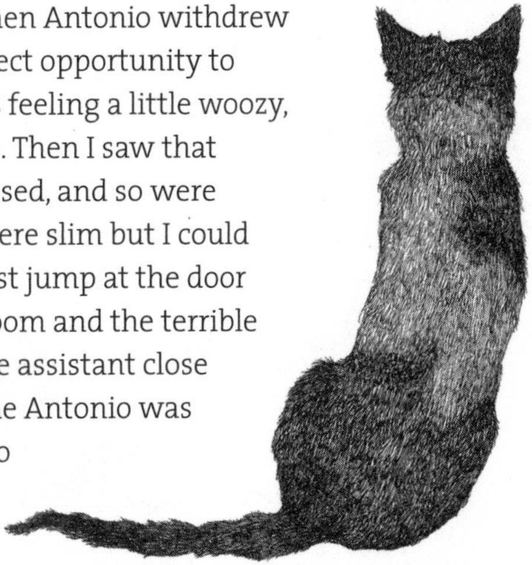

All the while, I was getting wobblier on my paws, but I wasn't any the less determined.

The next thing I knew, Antonio flew in my direction with the syringe in his hand like Billy the Kid. I could see anger flashing in his eyes. I had no choice but to aim for the side table that held all the medical equipment and I flew at it with all my might. The tray went crashing to the floor, and a glass bottle tumbled, smashing close to the tray. It all happened so fast, things went flying all over the place – implements fell down the side of the cabinet, more glass was breaking. I was doing a really good job of trashing the place,' 3jabs grinned.

'All of a sudden – wham! – he got me, right in the rear hind quarter. This time the pain was excruciating. Within seconds I was feeling drowsy, and completely unsteady. All I thought about was not giving in. I fought the sedative with so much determination.' 3jabs stopped for a breather as his audience waited, captivated. Poohka's mouth had dropped open, waiting for the climax of the story, even though he knew what was to come. 'As I tried to jump up at the door handle, it seemed to move,' he continued, slightly less dramatically. 'I was becoming more unsteady by the minute and found that I could not jump – my right back leg kept giving way. What was I to do?'

'What did you do, 3jabs?' cried Tigs, his paws at his cheeks in horror.

'Before I knew it, another syringe was plunged into my left side, and suddenly my body became numb. But I refused to close my eyes and I could see Antonio and Anya bearing down on me. I just about heard Antonio's voice say, "We'd better get this job done quickly, before this maniac comes around." Then everything became a blur! I do vaguely remember being dumped back into the wooden box, and the door slammed shut. The remains of the sardines were starting to smell a little rancid, but I was so out of it, I did not care. I closed my eyes, and fell into the deepest of sleeps. That is the last I remember of that awful day.'

Poohka, Tigs and the other cats all gasped as 3jabs's story came to an end. But he hadn't quite finished.

'The following afternoon,' 3jabs went on, chuckling, 'I was collected by another lady from the estate, Annabel, and her husband Alex. I heard Antonio explain to them that it had taken three injections to knock me out, and even then I was not completely under. He also told them I had caused absolute havoc and ruined his surgery, so he never wanted to see me again! As I was carried into Annabel and Alex's car I breathed a huge sigh of relief. Then I concentrated on what they were saying as Alex turned the key to start the engine. Before taking his foot off the brake, he looked at Annabel and said, "I think we should call him 3jabs. What do you think?" "I think it is the perfect name for him," replied Annabel, smiling. And so that is why I am affectionately named 3jabs.' 3jabs grinned to himself as his story finally came to a close.

Poohka rolled over and stretched out to his fullest length in awe of his friend 3jabs. Poohka closed his eyes and thought of how lucky he was to have such a beautiful place to live, with such wonderful friends. Especially his greatest friend of all, 3jabs. But his friends weren't all cats. He loved his daily walks with Alex and Annabel around the villas of Sotogrande. Life could not be better. In fact, it was perfect!

As the other cats wandered off, Poohka felt a grumble in his stomach. 'I'm feeling a little peckish,' he realised.

'Go and check out the dustbins outside the entrance of the estate,' said 3jabs. 'I got a good whiff of some prawns when I passed by earlier. Normally I would have been tempted to take a look and sample the delights, but I had a good night's hunting and am ready for my siesta.' And, with that, 3jabs yawned, then closed his eyes to take a nap.

Poohka had another good, slow stretch, then got to his feet and meandered in the direction of the rubbish bins. 'Wow, prawns,' Poohka said in a whisper. 'My favourite.'

As he arrived at the large refuse containers, the smell of prawns was quite overpowering. Poohka's heart missed a beat at the prospect of the feast to come.

He climbed up a discarded carpet that was propped against a cardboard box beside the rubbish bins, then leapt up on to the top of the bin. He immediately started rummaging through the contents to get to the source of the fishy smells. But there were no prawns in here.

Undeterred, Poohka jumped into the next-door rubbish skip. And there they were! Nestled in a corner, a big bag full of discarded prawn shells.

'This will keep me busy for the rest of the afternoon!' Poohka thought to himself, thrilled at his find. Siesta time would have to wait – this was far more important.

Poohka was surprised that he was the only one around the dustbin area. Normally, if his chums had caught a whiff of the prawns, they would be in the bin alongside him, consuming the delights before they were all gone.

'Never mind,' he thought. 'This means they are all for me – how wonderful is that?' Poohka, unable to contain himself, started to purr loudly, as he scavenged the prawns and satisfied his growling stomach.

Soon, Poohka came across one really large untouched prawn. It was full of juicy meat, but as he picked it up in his jaws, he slipped on the can where he had placed his left paw. The delicious prawn fell from his mouth and slipped down into the pile of rubbish inside the container. Poohka wasn't about to let such a juicy prawn go, and began pawing his way deeper into the skip.

All of a sudden, the whole container moved! It lurched sideways, tipping Poohka out of the rubbish bin into an even bigger container full of hundreds of bin bags. He leapt up, struggled desperately to get to his feet amongst the rubbish, and saw the bin he'd first climbed into hanging perilously above him. He knew he had to get out before the contents of this one were poured on top of him. But he could not move fast enough, and his meows went unheard. Rubbish poured down as Poohka heard the first skip crashing back into place on the ground, with the next one only moments behind.

Poohka, terrified, tried hopelessly to scramble to the top of the rubbish, but just as fast as he climbed, more containers of rubbish were emptied on to him. He meowed as loudly as he could. Surely someone would hear him? Alas, no one did! The rubbish machine made so much noise that nothing could be heard by the dustmen doing their Sotogrande round.

As the claws of the machine began to whip around the rubbish, Poohka tumbled back and forth to avoid the mechanical pincers, desperately grabbing at anything that might help to save him. He was hot, scared and running out of energy. Just when he thought he could scramble no longer, Poohka found a large black bin liner containing something very solid – solid enough to protect him from the giant claws – and he propped himself next to it. Exhausted, Poohka collapsed beside it.

Panting heavily to get his breath back, Poohka put a solitary paw up to his face. Then it hit him. Of course! It was Wednesday – rubbish day! The day everyone knew to stay well clear of the rubbish bins. No wonder no other cats were around!

'I was so consumed with hunger, I forgot what day it was,' Poohka told himself. Then he slumped back, and suddenly everything went black.

Chapter 2 - No place for a siesta

In August, the hottest time of the year in southern Spain, Spike sat motionless in the heat of the sun. He was perched on a decaying branch of an old cork oak tree. The week had passed too slowly for Spike, a mature and splendid looking vulture. Spike longed for Wednesdays to come around, and waited impatiently.

There was a gentle but obvious roar of a lorry in the distance. Spike jumped up, stretched his scaly neck and flexed his claws. 'It's coming!' he cried joyfully.

Señor Arbol, the once majestic cork oak tree, groaned loudly. 'For goodness' sake, Spike, if you carry on with this behaviour you will break my weary old branch. Then you will lose your prime spot here at the rubbish tip.'

'OK, OK!' he yelled with excitement, struggling to contain himself. 'I'll try my best, but my tummy is rumbling so much, and my food is on its way!'

As if in reply, the decaying branch beneath Spike made a big creaking noise. Spike gulped and immediately stopped bouncing up and down. Spike liked his vantage point closest to the dumping area, and he'd fought hard to get this prime position. He had no intention of losing it now!

As the lorry made its way along the parched, uneven surface of the landfill site, it jerked up and down and side to side. Both Señor Arbol and Spike could feel the vibration of the vehicle as it came nearer.

Spike could barely contain himself when the lorry stopped close to the old cork tree. The branch creaked loudly once more. Señor Arbol let out yet another big sigh.

All of a sudden, heads popped up from the mounds of rubbish already scattered across the landfill site. All eyes were fixed on the lorry about to dump its load. Squeals of excitement echoed around as the smells from the rubbish drifted through the air.

The driver and his assistants climbed down from the cab and set to work. The smells grew stronger as the crushed contents of the lorry were tipped up and over – exposed for all to see. The men climbed quickly back up into the driver's cab and the door slammed closed. Within seconds the noisy lorry moved away over the bumpy ground, its chains clanging against the empty container. As it turned out of the site, turning right onto the main road heading south, peace returned to the site of the newly dumped rubbish.

Within an instant, all sorts of creatures appeared from nowhere. They all had the same desire: to have a long-awaited meal. A feast of all feasts!

But Spike was the first to swoop down on top of the new rubbish. He ripped and pecked his way furiously through the bin bags, eating everything edible in his path.

All the rats, mice and other animals knew only too well to stay clear of Spike. He could not be trusted – before you knew it, you could be his next meal. Spike would eat anything – dead or alive!

Raimondo was a lazy, overweight individual, and head of the rat fraternity. He exploited his position as Chief Rat – especially on Wednesdays. Raimondo wandered over to the newly dumped rubbish, careful to stay clear of Spike. He was in search of his rat underlings in order to feast on the best pickings they had already unravelled.

Just then, a junior rat, Paco, was celebrating his find: a banana skin brunch to end all brunches!

'Thanks, Paco,' Raimondo said as he approached. 'You can move on now to another area until I am done here.' The Chief Rat began munching the tasty banana skin.

'Right you are, boss' said Paco, without hesitation. 'Come

on, kids, let's move down the pile,' he added glumly. 'We'll get some food there if we are lucky.' So Paco and his family moved obediently along.

Raimondo was already well into Paco's leftovers and ate the lot with gusto. After a few burps and sighs of delight, Raimondo eventually wiped his whiskers with his front paws, rolled over and let out a big yawn. Now that his stomach was full to the brim, it was time to take a much-needed siesta. Raimondo tweaked his whiskers, gave his tummy a good scratch, closed both eyes and promptly fell asleep.

As soon as Raimondo's snores rang out, Paco and his family could go back to scavenging without fear of interruption. Paco had to find as much as he could to keep his family going. The population was growing here at the rubbish dump, and no one knew if there would be enough food to go around in the months to come.

Señor Arbol watched the scene unfold feeling very tired and weary. He could remember the days when he was the focus of a wonderful estate, greatly admired by estate owners throughout the country. But sadly, times had changed, and the estate was now used as a landfill site.

What's more, Señor Arbol knew his own days were numbered. What he wanted more than anything was for the rains to come to quench his thirst. He only had a small supply of water stashed away for emergencies, and he wondered if he could survive the month of August with the sun beating down so fiercely. His branches were badly scorched as was the outer layer of cork around his trunk.

As he surveyed the scurrying animals, Señor Arbol thought he saw something unusual out of the corner of his eye. Of course there was a lot of activity going on within the enormous pile of rubbish, but something inside made him feel that this was important.

Señor Arbol strained to see what it was that had caught his attention, and saw a head rise from a black bin liner. As the head fell slowly back down, it knocked a tin can, and a jingling sound rang out. Most of the animals stopped for a moment before they quickly resumed their meals.

Nearby, Spike was far too intent on ripping open bags and boxes to notice the noise. But as the tin can rolled down the heap of rubbish, Señor Arbol knew it was his duty to do something. 'Raimondo,' he called in his deep, melancholy voice.

Raimondo opened one eye, then promptly closed it. He was not going to let anyone disturb his much-needed siesta!

'Raimondo, this is important!' called Señor Arbol. This time his voice was low but showed more determination and urgency.

'What do you want? I am trying to have a well-earned siesta,' replied Raimondo.

'I need your help. Raimondo, please!' pleaded Señor Arbol.

Raimondo had been woken from one of his wonderful dreams, and was about to curl up to go back to sleep, when he remembered that it was Señor Arbol who had saved his life not all that long ago, when he too had ended up on the rubbish tip.

'OK, OK, what is it?' Raimondo reluctantly replied. 'This had better be important. I do not take kindly to being woken from a good dream!'

'I have seen some unusual movement in the lower left quarter, not far from Spike,' said Señor Arbol. 'I think it may be an animal in distress. Please try and stir the little creature, then get it over to me as quickly as possible before Spike becomes aware of anything.'

'How come you always give me the easy jobs?' Raimondo murmured sarcastically.

Señor Arbol ignored the rat. 'If Spike knows what is going on, the injured animal will not stand a chance, so you must be quick, but please also be careful.'

'OK, OK, I will get on to it, pronto!' gasped Raimondo.

The Chief Rat began climbing the pile of rubbish that Señor Arbol had indicated, not far away from Spike.

Fortunately, Spike was still totally immersed in devouring all sorts of unsavoury things in his area, oblivious to anything else going on around him. However, Raimondo was aware this could change in a second.

Raimondo's eyesight was pretty good, but as he approached he couldn't see any sign of a little animal in distress. Raimondo did not dare get any closer, as it would draw attention to himself as well as to whatever Señor Arbol had seen.

If Spike realised something was going on, he would raise the alarm, then his whole ghastly family would descend on the landfill site and they'd all be in really big trouble! The thought sent shivers down Raimondo's spine, conjuring up a terrifying vision of Spike and all his relatives pecking away at both him and his troop of rats, not to mention the injured animal he was trying to save.

But perhaps it was already too late for the creature buried within the rubbish?

Raimondo started tapping the small tin can tied to his neck to send out his emergency signal to all his fellow able-bodied rodents. Within seconds, over fifty strong rats surrounded him, ready for instructions.

'Paco,' Raimondo said, 'there's an injured animal out there who needs my help. I need you to take your group over to Spike and cause a disturbance. You must keep Spike distracted long enough for the rest of us to get to the left-hand quarter and to that damsel in distress,' explained Raimondo.

'We're on to it, Chief!' Paco cried, then immediately scampered off in Spike's direction with his group of rats.

Once Paco's group were in place, Raimondo and his group moved swiftly towards the lower left-hand quarter, dodging plastic bags, tin cans, string, ripped cardboard boxes and all sorts of other discarded rubbish. Eventually, Raimondo came to a halt; he'd spotted a bundle of matted, dirty ginger fur amongst the piles.

Raimondo's heart sank. He had desperately hoped he'd be saving a beautiful lady rat. Instead it appeared to be something much bigger.

He turned to the rat by his side, a grey-furred rodent named Pedro. 'Pedro, hold the troops back at a distance. I will go in to check out this creature first. We cannot be too careful.'

Pedro nodded. 'Be on your guard, Raimondo,' he replied. 'We will be ready for all eventualities.'

'Thanks, Pedro, I know I can trust you,' said a worried Raimondo.

Spike was still happily devouring all kinds of goodies. He was currently enjoying a half-eaten chicken and some delicious potatoes coated with scrumptious custard. His eyes rolled with delight when, all of a sudden, up popped Paco and his gang of rats. Before Spike could chase them away, they started throwing at him any sort of rubbish they could get their paws on.

'Get away, you horrible rats, or I will gobble you all up!' Spike cried out. 'If you are not careful, I will coat you in some delicious custard and add you to my dinner!' Spike was getting angrier by the second; he had no intention of abandoning the latest treasure of goodies he'd unravelled from a luxury carrier bag!

'Keep throwing things at him,' called Paco to his fellow rats, 'until I give the all-clear.'

So the barrage continued, and Spike got angrier and angrier. But he didn't want to retaliate and lose his precious bag of goodies in the process.

Although the thought of custard-coated rat did not

overwhelm him, Spike decided it was time to take some action. He could use the pile of clean bones neatly stacked at his side as weapons, and began to shower the rats with the chicken bones. He grinned as, one by one, the rats retreated down the rubbish pile, ducking and dodging the missiles being hurled at them from a height.

Spike was beginning to wonder if he'd need to call on his family of vultures for assistance, but that would definitely mean forfeiting his gourmet meal!

Then, as suddenly as they had appeared, the gang of rats backed off, and had soon completely disappeared from sight.

'Thank heavens for that!' Spike sighed with delight. He quickly returned to gorging himself on the feast in the bag before anyone or anything could take it away.

Raimondo moved cautiously towards the mound of ginger mess. He first poked his nose and then his feet into the motionless bundle of fur.

'Nothing happening here,' said Raimondo. 'I think he's a goner. I'll remove some of the debris on top to investigate further.'

'Be careful, Chief,' called Pedro from a distance.

'Don't worry, I will,' gasped Raimondo. 'I am not enjoying this one little bit.'

Raimondo began digging away the rubbish around the matted ginger and white fur. Suddenly he froze.

'What is it, Chief?' cried Pedro.

'It's a CAT!' shrieked the Chief Rat.

Pedro and his troop of rats shuffled further back at this revelation. They'd risked their lives trying to save a CAT. Their number one enemy!

'Bring the cat to me,' boomed Señor Arbol.

Raimondo spun around. 'You must be kidding,' he said. 'This is not a rescue I want to be part of.'

Señor Arbol sighed. 'You must help the creature, Raimondo. Please bring it to me as quickly as possible.'

Raimondo stared at the matted fur, until eventually guilt got the better of him. He started to prod the cat, hoping it was either dead or in a coma. Raimondo wanted to get out of this predicament as soon as he could, return to his cosy home and get on with his siesta!

The cat still showed no sign of life. Raimondo was reluctant to get too close to the cat's head for fear of waking it and ending up as its dinner.

The Chief Rat signalled with a paw to Señor Arbol. 'I cannot do this. It's way beyond the call of duty.'

'Please, Raimondo, if the cat is still alive, just bring the little mite to me, and you will be free of it. Remember, I once did the same for you.'

'But what if I help save this cat only to be eaten by it, once it's back to health? No, thank you!' Raimondo shouted. 'Pick another sucker; I quit!'

Raimondo turned to his gang. 'Come on, lads, let's get out of here. A rat saving a cat – you must be joking.' The rat started to walk away, but then stopped in his tracks. He'd seen the cat's chest move. 'It's breathing!' he gulped.

'All the more reason to save it!' sighed Señor Arbol. 'I am very disappointed in you, Raimondo. I thought you were a better rat than that. If you let the cat die without even trying to save it, it will be on your conscience for the rest of your life. Can you live with that?'

Raimondo knew Señor Arbol was a wise old tree, but this wasn't what he wanted to hear right at this moment. He couldn't care less for the cat, but he did care about Señor Arbol.

Raimondo took a deep breath, and spun on his heels. 'OK, troops, we're back on the job again,' he gasped. 'But nobody wake the cat, otherwise we'll all be for it.'

Pedro and his fellow rats crept closer and closer to the animal. They surrounded its furry body and, in unison, very gently lifted the motionless creature. Carrying their greatest enemy, they inched slowly towards Señor Arbol, trying to avoid tin cans, rubbish and anything else in their paths that might make enough noise to wake their dangerous load.

But Pedro was looking ahead to the great cork oak tree and didn't see a decaying banana skin poking out from the rubbish. He stumbled and lost his grip on the cat's head! An almighty gasp went out from all the rats carrying the animal and then they froze in fear.

Pedro slowly reached down to the cat's head and lifted it back up in his trembling paws. 'It's, err, OK, err, lads,' he said in a stuttering voice. 'The cat is still unconscious but let's move on quickly.'

The rats let out a great sigh when eventually they reached the base of Señor Arbol's trunk.

As soon as they'd released the still-motionless creature, the rats darted off in the direction of the new pile of rubbish without waiting for any more orders. Back to scavenging once more!

Raimondo quickly sent out a signal via his tin can that the job was now terminated – the rats could get back to their previous activities, well away from Spike. Finally, Raimondo could resume his siesta, and he did so easily, falling gently into the land of nod and dreaming about faraway places after a job well done – albeit for a cat!

Meanwhile, as night fell, Señor Arbol tended the little ginger cat, becoming more concerned with the condition of the injured animal curled up at the bottom of his tree trunk. Although he could feel breathing coming from the cat, there were no other signs of life.

Señor Arbol desperately wanted to keep the animal alive. He felt responsible for the animals around him, and after all the rats' efforts to deliver the cat, he could not give up now! But Señor Arbol's powers were limited and the recent drought had reduced him to living off his emergency supply of water.

He soon realised he had no choice – he would have to give the cat what little fluids he still had, whatever the consequences to himself.

He focused on sending all the fluid in his branches down through his trunk to the outer coating of cork, by which the comatose animal lay. Then with one great, final effort, he squeezed the fluid out of the cork right into the cat's mouth.

As he passed on his 'elixir of life', Señor Arbol felt his whole trunk shudder, then wither a little more. His energies fell considerably, but he knew this was the only chance he had to save one of God's creatures.

It was now very clear to Señor Arbol that if the rains did not come soon, his life would be over.

Chapter 3 - Time to wake up

Poohka felt cold, tired and strange. Where was he? He didn't dare open his eyes, but he twitched his ears. He could hear the rustling of tree leaves, but he had no idea where he was. Very slowly, he opened his eyes. 'Where am I?' said his squeaky, scared voice.

'You are safe, little one, for the time being,' said the low, tired voice of the cork oak tree that towered above him. 'I am Señor Arbol, and I will help get you well again and on your way as soon as possible.'

'This must be a terrible dream!' squealed Poohka. 'I live in Sotogrande – a beautiful place. This is just a h-h-horrible nightmare,' stuttered the cat.

'I am sorry, little one, for this is not a bad dream. You are in a landfill site, where all the rubbish is dumped, far away from your beautiful home,' whispered Señor Arbol.

Poohka felt a tear roll slowly from his eye and along his whiskers, dropping onto his lips. He licked it away and shook his head.

'What is your name, little one?' asked Señor Arbol.

Poohka was scared, but the old cork tree seemed trustworthy. 'It's Poohka, sir. Please, what am I to do? I must get home, back to Sotogrande.' He could feel himself shaking, but he knew it was not just from the cold.

'I will see what I can do to help you find your way home, but it will not be easy,' whispered Señor Arbol. 'There are many dangerous creatures here and so you must not stay long. I do have one friend I can trust but I am not sure if he will be prepared to help. The problem is that you are a cat!' Señor Arbol sighed, his voice getting ever fainter with his diminishing strength. 'Unfortunately you felines do not have any friends amongst the vermin or birds around these parts of Andalucía. But get some rest, and we will see what tomorrow brings.'

As Señor Arbol became silent, Poohka let out a sigh of desperation. What was he to do? He could not stay here in this terrifying, dirty place. The smells were overwhelming and his body hurt all over.

'How on earth did I get here?' he asked himself. 'This has to be a dream – a very BAD dream. If I close my eyes for a few minutes then maybe when I reopen them I will be back with my friends at home.'

Poohka squeezed his eyes shut for a good ten minutes. But when he flashed them open wide once more he was still in the worst place on earth: a rubbish dump. What's more, he could see gleaming eyes glaring at him from the piles of rubbish. Poohka had never felt so scared or alone.

It was all very well for Señor Arbol to tell him to get some sleep – but how could he? Poohka felt battered and bruised – every part of his body hurt – and worst of all he didn't have the memory to put the pieces together. How on earth had he ended up here in this dangerous place, when only hours ago he was listening to his great friend 3jabs telling his tales in the beautiful gardens at the estate?

'Come on, Poohka, try to remember!' the cat said to himself. 'What did you do after you listened to 3jabs?' But it was no good. He had no clue how he got here. 'What is the point?' he gasped, realising the danger he was in. 'It is not going to get me out of here. I've got to get to safer surroundings. I have to get home.'

Poohka tried to summon the energy to get up, but his head throbbed and he hurt everywhere. The most excruciating pain came from his front left leg. As he tried to lift himself up, his leg buckled underneath him and he heard an almighty CRACK! The pain shot through his body and he dropped to the ground, defeated.

He had no idea whether the old tree was still listening, but Poohka said in the weakest of voices, 'Señor Arbol, I don't think I can go anywhere. I've broken my leg and I will not be able to find my way home now – my life is over. Please leave me to die.'

Poohka closed his eyes again, abandoning all hope of ever returning to his beloved home and friends in Sotogrande. As sleep took him, he hoped that he'd never wake up again.

Chapter 4 - The journey begins

By noon the next day Señor Arbol had become increasingly concerned for Poohka. There had been no sign of any life from him in the many hours since nightfall. But the old cork tree was not about to give up just yet.

While Poohka slept, Señor Arbol had been putting some plans into place. He'd arranged for his friend Señor Buho to help the little cat on his journey back to Sotogrande. The problem was going to be persuading Poohka that he was strong enough to make the journey.

'Poohka, Poohka, if you are awake please answer my call,' Señor Arbol asked for the hundredth time, or so it seemed.

Señor Arbol drew in a breath as Poohka stirred, and spoke very softly. 'Please let me die; I cannot go on. I will never be able to make it home.'

'Now pull yourself together, you are a young, strong cat,' said Señor Arbol in a low, firm voice. 'You only have a broken leg. You must be positive – with the right amount of willpower you can achieve whatever you wish for.'

Poohka had gone quiet again, but Señor Arbol knew he was listening. 'My good friend, Señor Buho, a wise old owl, is prepared to help you on your journey back to Sotogrande. So you had better show some respect and lighten up,' commanded Señor Arbol. 'You will be leaving at nightfall, so it is very important you muster up all your strength and the commitment to make the long journey home. Señor Buho has only agreed to assist you on condition you do exactly as he says,' continued Señor Arbol. 'You are fortunate that he knows Sotogrande, and he can take you there via the shortest route. You could not have a better guide than Señor Buho.'

Poohka did not respond for some time. He was still getting over the shock of the events of the last two days. But he knew he had two choices: to stay where he was and die alone in this terrible place, or to pull himself together and at least attempt to make the journey back home.

'I can do it,' Poohka murmured to himself. 'I will show 3jabs how strong and courageous I am. Yes, I will do it!'

Poohka opened his eyes wide at Señor Arbol. 'I am going home!' he cried.

'I am very pleased to hear it,' sighed Señor Arbol. 'Already, many animals have gone out of their way to save you. Being strong and determined is the least you can do for them.' His voice shook with exhaustion as he spoke. 'Now, you must take a siesta so you are well rested, and be ready to depart at dusk. Being an owl, Señor Buho can only travel at night,' he explained.

But Poohka could not sleep. He was so excited about the prospect of going home and suddenly felt like the journey was possible after all. His left leg hurt a lot, but he resolved to get used to it and try to block it out.

Señor Buho, the wise old owl, landed promptly on Señor Arbol's branch just as the sun sank into the horizon. 'Come on, young lad, chop-chop, we have plenty of ground to cover tonight before daylight returns,' Señor Buho commanded.

'It is very kind of you to assist me, Señor Buho. My name is Poohka,'

the cat introduced himself politely.

Señor Buho shook out his wings. 'There is no time for formalities – that can be done on our journey. For now we must leave, sharpish!' he demanded.

'Good luck, Poohka,' whispered Señor Arbol. 'It is time for you to depart. Señor Buho is a good and very wise friend of mine, and he will help you on your way to Sotogrande. For your safety, please do exactly as he says.'

At that, Señor Buho took flight, his wings expanding fully before flapping purposefully into the still of the night.

Poohka lifted himself onto his three good legs. The fourth leg dangled uselessly – he would have to limp his way home.

'Take care, Poohka. Farewell, my friend. Have a safe journey home,' sighed Señor Arbol faintly.

Poohka stopped abruptly and turned his head back to Señor Arbol. 'Thank you, Señor Arbol, for saving me. Goodbye!' Then Poohka limped a little faster, eager to catch up with Señor Buho.

The wise owl heard Poohka behind him in the distance, and realised he was some way ahead of his charge. He flew back and descended directly above Poohka, wings flapping. 'SILENCE, or you will attract all kinds of evil creatures,' he said in a stern voice. 'We have no time to lose, so hurry up!'

As they moved forwards, Poohka couldn't help but give a heavy sigh. He was finding it impossible to keep up with the owl's pace – his front left leg was just dangling and he had no control over it. What's more, it hurt so much. But Poohka forced himself to rise above the excruciating pain and think only of getting home to Sotogrande. With great determination and all of his strength, he moved as fast as his three legs would take him.

Raimondo and his fellow rats were doing their usual evening search through the piles of rubbish. It was the safest time to explore for treasure and food as Spike did not venture onto the tip at night.

Raimondo had just seen the cat leaving with Señor Buho, struggling to keep up on his three legs. 'Thank goodness the cat has left – that's one less danger to worry about!' he thought to himself. Raimondo returned to his rummaging and the welfare of the cat became the furthest thing from his mind.

Not so Señor Arbol, who could just about make out Señor Buho above Poohka at the gates of the rubbish dump. He knew Señor Buho would keep his word, guiding Poohka on his journey home to Sotogrande. Although he was not sure how Poohka would take to Señor Buho, he hoped the brave little cat would do as the wise owl said and get home safely.

As Señor Arbol prayed for the rains to come and revive him, he whispered a final farewell in the wind: 'Goodbye, Poohka, my little friend.'

Chapter 5 - A long, hard night

By the time Poohka had reached the gates to the refuse site he was exhausted and in desperate need of some water. The young cat had found it very hard to keep up with Señor Buho – the ground was so uneven, full of potholes, and at night it was especially difficult to see them all. Every now and again he stumbled and fell. Poohka could tell Señor Buho was getting even more annoyed with his slow progress.

'This is not working,' muttered Señor Buho gruffly. 'You are not keeping up with me, and we have many miles to cover before daylight. You will have to make more of an effort or I give up!'

'I am sorry, Señor Buho, but I am doing my very best. I cannot control my broken leg and I am finding it so painful. Now we have passed the potholes and we have reached the main road it will be easier. I will do my upmost to keep up with you. Maybe if you flew ahead and waited on a branch in the distance, I could catch up – then we could do the same again, and again?' Poohka suggested.

'But we are not travelling on the main road. The shortest route is across the olive groves heading towards the forest in the distance,' the owl said.

Poohka nodded. He'd have to try to keep up with Señor Buho's pace.

After a while he slowed again.

'What now?' Señor Buho squawked.

'I am very thirsty,' explained Poohka.

The owl flapped his wings. 'OK – I will check out a water supply for you en route.'

Señor Buho was soon perched on a rusty but rather grand gate at the edge of an estate. Poohka looked up hopefully. Señor Buho pointed his wing at a hut just inside the gate. Beside it was an old water trough. Poohka hobbled over, but however much he tried he couldn't get up to look in the trough. He couldn't even jump up onto the ledge to see the water, let alone drink what little liquid might be inside. Despair flooded over him. Poohka would have to wait until he could find water elsewhere.

'I cannot reach it,' he sighed.

Señor Buho let out an even bigger sigh and flew off into the distance. Poohka didn't know what to do – Señor Buho was flying much faster than before.

Just as the little cat was beginning to think Señor Buho had left him for good, he spotted the great owl in the dark sky with a small plastic container in his beak. Had Señor Buho gone all the way back to the rubbish tip to find it?

Poohka looked up and licked his lips as Señor Buho perched on the side of the trough, then flew down and scooped up some water into the pot. He landed close to Poohka and set the cup awkwardly on the ground. 'Now hurry up and drink the water. We have no time to lose. At this rate we will never make it to the forest before daylight.'

Poohka hurriedly drank the water to quench his thirst as Señor Buho flew towards the olive trees in the distance. Within no time at all Poohka was moving as fast as he possibly could on his three good legs.

Señor Buho sat on an olive branch, waiting for Poohka. The cat guessed that he'd been there a long time. 'Go behind the olive tree, and you will find some food I have collected for you. But be quick about it,' Señor Arbol said sternly.

Poohka's heart missed a beat. 'Food, what a wonderful surprise!' he thought to himself.

But when he set eyes on his meal his heart sank. Sitting behind the tree were some squashed, dried-up insects – he wasn't sure exactly what. This was not what Poohka called food!

He couldn't bring himself to eat it.

'You have not eaten anything!' exclaimed Señor Buho as Poohka continued to stare at the insects.

'Thank you, but I am not hungry,' Poohka replied politely.

'So you are a fussy eater too! You cannot waste such good food.' Señor Buho promptly swooped down and consumed the squashed insects. 'It is time to be on our way, otherwise we will never get to safety before daybreak,' commanded Señor Buho once more.

Poohka felt very weak and his leg hurt badly, but he knew he had to persevere otherwise he may never make it home. He thought about being back with his friends and wished that this terrible pain would go away.

The night seemed long and endless and Poohka had a lot of trouble walking. His limp, broken leg dangled so much that Poohka kept knocking it, and soon it began to bleed. Poohka was leaving a small trail of blood as he went. This was no good – he couldn't leave tracks which might put him in even greater danger. Poohka had no choice but to stop occasionally to lick the blood from the wound.

The night got even darker, and Poohka could hear wolves howling in the distance. Strange-sounding noises came from the trees, but Poohka didn't ask Señor Buho what they were. He wanted to be as brave as possible and make it safely to the forest before the sun rose.

In the early light of day Poohka could see Señor Buho perched on an old tree stump, a little way ahead. Poohka had no energy left, and would have to tell the owl soon that he needed to rest – he was so very, very tired. But as Poohka approached the stump he could see Señor Buho looked extremely cross, and knew it was because of their lack of progress. The young cat refrained from saying anything until he had heard what Señor Buho had to say.

'This is totally unacceptable, Poohka. We cannot make any headway unless you make more of an effort,' bleated Señor Buho. 'I am wasting my time here and morning is breaking. I need to be safe in the forest now, to rest until our next passage tonight.'

Poohka felt bad – he'd tried his hardest, but Señor Buho was clearly angry that it had taken him so long to walk this far.

'Make your way over to the forest in the distance,' Señor Buho continued. 'I will be ready to start once again when night falls. And make sure you get some rest today, as we have many more miles to cover tonight. You will never get back home otherwise.' With that, Señor Buho opened his wings and soared high up into the sky towards the forest in the distance.

Poohka stood frozen in horror. He had not been able to say a word and now his protector was gone. 'How on earth am I going to get to the forest quickly, to have a good rest before we continue again tonight?' he thought. The forest loomed ahead on the horizon, a mass of brown trees, burnt by the sun. Poohka guessed it would take him many hours to reach it. He didn't have time!

Poohka looked instead at the row of olive trees close by. He'd rest in one of those trees for now, and be refreshed enough in a few hours to continue to the forest. When he reached the trees he began to circle one, seeking out the right branch to head for, one that would be safe from predators and also sheltered from the sun when it had risen. But there was one problem. When he tried to climb up the tree, his broken leg got in the way.

Back in Sotogrande, he used to climb trees all the time – now he felt useless. He couldn't even climb this tiny olive tree.

Poohka collapsed at the base of the tree. What was he to do? His heart was pounding, his head was thumping, and he needed to find a safe place to sleep. There was only one solution. He had to keep going until he made it to the forest entrance where he would be safer. Only then could he rest.

The solitary journey was long and arduous as the sun rose higher in the sky. Soon, the birds of prey were flying above in circles, looking for something to feast on!

Poohka tried with all his might to raise his damaged leg, and hobbled on his three legs as fast as they would take him. The cat willed himself on as the vultures continued to circle above him, every now and then descending low enough to remind Poohka just how close they were. Poohka limped on in fear for his life.

By mid-morning, the sun was beating down and Poohka was thirstier and hotter than ever. But he could not give up now or all would be lost. The vulture family were now circling even closer to him, swooping down every now and then as though playing a very nasty game.

Poohka knew they only had one thing in mind but he was determined not to let them have their way. He'd come this far already. Poohka was not going to be on their menu today – or any other day – so he summoned greater courage than ever before and continued to hobble on his way from one olive tree to the next. The trees not only protected him from the swooping predators but also from the heat of the sun.

Poohka was in dire need of water and felt close to collapse but he dared not leave the safety of the olive trees. Then he realised something – the vultures had given up! No longer were they circling in the blue sky above. 'Hoorah,' he thought, 'at last they have gone!' But wait – what was that? Poohka noticed one very large stray vulture above him, circling lower and lower.

Poohka was almost at the forest – but his heart was racing. How could he move from the last olive tree to his final destination in the dense forest just ahead? Then he spotted some aloe vera plants between him and the forest. Could they possibly give him some cover before he made a final dash for the forest? Poohka looked up again and saw the solitary vulture circling above. Adrenaline surged through his body and gave him a sudden burst of energy.

This was going to be the most dangerous part of his journey so far. How was he going to get to the aloe vera plants with a hungry vulture overhead watching his every move? The olive tree did not offer much protection either, so one way or another he would just have to make a dash for it. At least the spiky leaves of the aloe plant might be some protection for him. These were the thoughts that shot through his mind like rockets. He had no time to lose.

With one very deep breath, Poohka charged with all his might in the direction of the aloe vera plants. He tried to ignore the strong flapping sound of the vulture's wings above, growing louder by the second. He was only three metres away... now two... now one... but just as he reached out a paw for safety, Poohka felt claws dig into his back and he was lifted right off the ground.

'Oh no!' he thought. 'This is it, this is the end!'

Poohka could only hang in the air but, instead of rising, he realised they were getting closer to the ground again. The vulture was heading straight for a group of plants and struck the tallest plant, breaking a couple of its large spiky leaves.

The vulture let out an almighty shriek then Poohka felt its claws leave his back and he began to fall. Seconds later he crashed into the base of the plant and scrambled quickly to safety amidst its leaves. Peeking up, Poohka saw the vulture – missing a few feathers – flying off awkwardly in search of some other food.

Poohka licked himself down. He had a few extra scratches and many more bruises, but he couldn't believe he was still alive. He'd had a very lucky escape! Another scrape he had managed to come through. The cat let out an enormous sigh. 'Phew,' he thought, 'that was too close for comfort!'

Totally exhausted, Poohka instantly collapsed into a deep sleep. As he slept, the broken aloe vera leaves above him oozed their juices, some of which landed on his fur, and trickled gently into his sore mouth. Without knowing it, Poohka's thirst was being quenched and the juice also helped soothe his wound.

He wasn't sure how long he had dozed for, but when Poohka eventually came to, he felt a little boost of strength. His wound was less sore – in fact he had a soothing sensation all over. With renewed energy, in the late afternoon sun, Poohka limped the last strides to the forest, where he could get some rest away from danger before Señor Buho arrived at nightfall.

Chapter 6 - The old lady in the woods

When something pecked at Poohka's ear he jumped into the air in fright. Landing on the ground with a heavy thump, right on to his broken leg, he let out a cry of pain.

'Keep quiet, you lazy, good-for-nothing cat,' Señor Buho hissed. 'Do you want to get us both killed? There are some dangers in the forest, and we will not be completely safe until we get to the other side, closer to the white village several kilometres away.'

Poohka could barely hear a word Señor Buho was saying as an excruciating pain shot through his leg. It felt almost as if his leg had snapped in two.

Poohka's heart was pounding – he knew this was going to be a dangerous journey through the forest, and that Señor Buho was frustrated with him. He hoped that the forest was no worse than his experience across the barren olive groves while being hunted by vultures.

Poohka slowly lifted his body up, but it was clear he'd only be able to move at a very slow pace on his three remaining good legs in the forest undergrowth.

'I cannot move quickly, Señor Buho,' Poohka whispered.

'Well, that is a surprise,' said Señor Buho sarcastically. 'As if I have all the time in the world to get you to Sotogrande! I do have family of my own, you know.' Then he extended his magnificent wings and took off into the forest.

Poohka hobbled along through the rough ground, fearful of making too much noise and clenching his teeth to avoid crying out in pain.

'Where is this taking me?' he thought. 'Is it really worth it?' Dark questions kept running through his mind 'What is to become of me if I do finally make it back home to Sotogrande?'

Poohka's mind was suddenly distracted when he smelt some wonderful cooking aromas coming from deep within the forest.

'Do not go that way,' Señor Buho said in a very stern manner, flying low beside Poohka.

'But I am so hungry,' sighed Poohka. 'I am sure I can sneak a little bite to eat, then continue through the forest with you.'

A rustling sound came from behind the thorny bush ahead and, without warning, out stepped a small, plump woman. She stood directly in Poohka's path.

'I warned you,' quivered Señor Buho, taking flight immediately. 'I have to get away – see you on the other side of the forest when you eventually make it.'

Poohka stared after the wise owl for a moment, then turned back to the old lady. 'And where do you think you are going, my little fair one?' she said.

'I am on my way home to Sotogrande,' Poohka said nervously. 'I am very hungry, and I was trying to follow the wonderful smells coming from the forest.' Poohka hoped the old lady would feel sorry for him and allow him to continue on his way.

'So you're hungry, are you, my little one? Then you must come with me.' The old lady chuckled and stooped down, grabbing Poohka by the scruff of his neck and swinging him firmly under her right armpit. Poohka winced with pain, but remained silent.

After a few minutes, they'd arrived in front of a primitive, homemade house in the forest. 'Welcome to my humble dwelling, little one. Please make yourself at home, and I will prepare you a wondrous meal.' The old lady kept chuckling to herself, like she was constantly laughing at a private joke.

At night in the depth of the forest it is quite cold, especially when compared to the scorching heat of the olive grove by day. So when the old lady dropped Poohka from her strong clasp and he landed on the floor by the open log fire, he was pleased for the warmth. But he was unable to stifle a little shriek of pain as his broken leg hit the floor.

'Oh, you poor little thing, that looks very nasty,' the old lady said as she grabbed at his injured leg.

'Ow, that hurts!' he exclaimed.

Without hesitation, the old lady pulled out a dirty, blood-stained piece of cloth from the front pocket of her apron, and wound it around Poohka's injured leg.

When the leg was bandaged, the old lady spoke again. 'I am Señora Bruja – and what is your name?' she asked.

'Oh, I am very pleased to meet you, Señora Bruja. I am Poohka from Sotogrande.' Poohka knew that all this kind Señora Bruja would hear were purrs and meows, but he continued all the same. 'Thank you for your very kind hospitality. I am so lucky to have met you.' Poohka realised it was the first time he'd purred since his frightening experience in the refuse lorry.

'You rest awhile while I prepare your meal of rabbit stew.' Señora Bruja smirked, the corner of her peeling dried lips curling up just the slightest bit at the ends and displaying a number of blackened teeth. Poohka guessed it was supposed to be a smile although she looked uglier than ever. But Poohka was not deterred, and the warmth from the fireplace and the thought of a proper meal was enough to keep him happy for the time being.

Poohka stretched out and made himself as comfortable as possible in front of the fire. His broken leg was throbbing like mad, but he felt content and happy for the first time in a long time and soon he would have a warm meal in his belly. But when he closed his eyes, all he could think of was why Señor Buho showed such alarm when seeing Señora Bruja.

Poohka decided that Señor Buho had obviously not known Señora Bruja very well, and although her appearance and mannerisms seemed rather threatening, Poohka felt sure she was a most charming old lady. And, so far, she had been the perfect hostess. Feeling cosy and completely at ease, Poohka fell asleep.

Poohka was happily dreaming of chasing butterflies back in Sotogrande when he felt a sharp prod in his bandaged broken leg. He winced with pain, and looked up to see Señora Bruja poking his bad leg with a stick.

'Are you awake?' she barked, not quite as a perfect hostess should do. 'Oh dear, is that your bad leg?' she chuckled. 'Here, eat this delicious food. It'll make you lovely and juicy and tender... I mean chubby and healthy, ready for forest adventures, and then you can go back to sleep for as long as you like. Hee, hee, hee, hee,' sneered the old lady.

The meal tasted delicious, and Poohka ate it without taking a break. Señora Bruja watched his every mouthful, even when he licked the bowl clean.

'That's right. Hee, hee, hee, hee,' she chuckled, attempting another blackened-tooth smile, content that Poohka had consumed all the sedative herbs she had added to his stew. Then she turned and walked back to dish up her own enormous bowl of stew from the large pot that simmered on the burner, unaware she had carelessly covered her own filthy plate with some of the very same, sleep-inducing herbs.

Poohka ignored the old lady's strange chuckling, and lifted his body carefully, extending his injured leg to ease the pain. He let out a contented purr. Finally he was warm, safe, and had a full, satisfied tummy. Before long he was in a deep, deep sleep, dreaming of his wonderful life back in Sotogrande with his friends.

Chapter 7 - Everyone's talking

Annabel and Alex left their apartment most days at around five o'clock to walk the grounds of the estate, and at the same time they'd feed the wild cats their quota of food.

Over the last few days, they'd missed Poohka joining them on their daily rounds. 'Poohka, Poohka!' Annabel called, still hopeful to see him once more, waiting for the charming ginger and white cat to bound up to her feet in anticipation of a good stroke. But Poohka was nowhere to be seen.

'Maybe he's been shut in one of the garages?' Annabel said to Alex. But they searched the garages and there was no sign of him.

After a few more days they began to lose hope, although Alex tried to be optimistic.

'Perhaps someone has given him a good home,' he suggested. 'Poohka was such a friendly cat, maybe someone has adopted him.'

'I do hope so,' Annabel replied. Their walks around the estate were not the same without the company of Poohka and his chirpy meows.

3jabs was equally glum. He was very concerned about his chum's disappearance, and he prayed to goodness his best friend had not been consumed by the refuse lorry the week before. The longer Poohka was gone, the more worried 3jabs became. The thought of never seeing Poohka again upset 3jabs more than he wanted to admit.

To keep himself occupied, 3jabs made enquiries among the animals in the area each day.

By night he would wander down to the coastal side of Sotogrande to find out if any of the other feral cats from the village had seen his dear friend. But it was always the same –

in the early hours of each morning 3jabs would return with his head bowed low. No one had seen or heard from Poohka since the previous Wednesday when he'd gone in search of prawns in the rubbish bins.

3jabs felt an enormous amount of guilt as he had been the one to tell Poohka of the prawns. He may have sent his best friend to his death!

Life would never be the same here without dear Poohka. All the feral cats were talking about this unusual disappearance of the much-loved cat. But after two weeks, those in Sotogrande – both humans and cats – realised that there was no way Poohka would be coming back. It left a big hole in many hearts.

Chapter 8 - The rescue attempt

Señor Buho flew back and forth within the forest. He had watched from a distance and saw Señora Bruja snatch Poohka under her arm and carry him off to her dwelling in the forest.

The sight of her had made Señor Buho's blood curdle and his heart pound as if it would burst. She had taken his brothers and sisters, and he hoped to get his revenge one day – but the memories still haunted him.

Now he must focus on saving Poohka from the wicked witch. He sincerely hoped Poohka had remembered his warnings about the dangers of the area, but he had no idea how he would rescue the cat from the evil Señora Bruja.

'Stop and think,' Señor Buho said to himself. 'Where there is a will, there is a way.' The last thing he wanted to do was to let Señor Arbol down after promising he would get Poohka back to Sotogrande. 'Firstly, I must find out if he is still alive.'

He flew down quietly to the window and hoped he would not be spotted as he fluttered outside. He saw Señora Bruja's back to the window, and she was busy tucking into a large dish filled with a steaming pile of food. But Señor Buho could see no sign of Poohka. He gasped. 'Please do not let it be Poohka she has on her plate!'

Señor Buho needed to get closer. The window ledge was so rotten he worried it might break, but he dug in with his talons anyway and stared inside.

At first he couldn't see anything else in the gloomy house. The window was dirty from many years of dust and grime. It would soon be time to call it a night – Señor Buho needed to get back to the safety of his own home before daylight. He would have to return as night fell, still hopeful of Poohka's survival.

But as he released his talons from the window sill and flapped his wings to take flight, he spotted something in the corner of his eye. A bundle of white and ginger fur just by the fireplace.

'Thank goodness,' he sighed. 'Poohka is still alive!'

Señor Buho had to leave before dawn, but he also wanted Poohka to know he would be back for him at dusk. He flew back down and landed gently on the rickety window sill.

'Owwww!' he cried silently, not wanting Señora Bruja to hear, as he pulled out one of his beautiful feathers with his beak. He wedged it gently into the rotten wood of the window frame. 'Poohka will recognise my feather when he wakes and looks up at the window, and he will know I am coming back for him.' Señor Buho extended his wings to their fullest and took off into the forest just as the sun threatened to poke over the horizon.

Meanwhile, Señora Bruja rubbed her bulging stomach after her meal of rabbit stew. 'Things are looking up,' she said to herself. 'Soon the cat will be fattened up and ready for eating. What a delicious meal that will be.' She turned to the cracked broken sink, and noticed a decaying mouse at its edge. She licked her lips and lifted it to her mouth, sliding the rotting creature in between her cracked, sore, seeping lips. First, she bit off its tail. Then, in one swallow, it was gone. She let out a thunderous belch before gulping down a cup of warmed leftover rabbit blood mixed with fermented berries.

Señora Bruja rose unsteadily from the table and staggered to her faithful old rickety chair, where she collapsed into the ripped upholstery. She landed on a protruding spring – 'Ouch!' – but soon settled back in a dizzy state of euphoria, overcome with drunkenness. Within minutes, Señora Bruja's long, loud snores were sending vibrations through her chair.

In the early hours of the morning Señor Buho had sent news to his family that he would not be returning home any time soon. His mission had incurred problems and he would have to remain in the forest until further notice.

Señor Buho had a fretful day dozing on and off. He was hidden within the branches above Señora Bruja's chimney stack, and anxious for nightfall. He had no idea if Poohka had survived the day as the wicked witch hadn't left her dwelling at all during the day.

The light was beginning to fade and Señor Buho could not wait a moment longer. Descending with speed, he flew down towards the rotten window ledge to look for signs of life. By now, he was less concerned whether Señora Bruja saw him or not – it was more important to check that Poohka was still alive. Landing heavily on the rotten wood, he lost his balance and crashed hard into the window. His heart missed several beats as he waited for the wicked witch to come storming through the front door of her house, straight into his path.

But as he steadied himself on the window ledge he heard no movement from inside. Through the filthy window, Señor Buho could make out the fire, which was dying down and emitting only a glimmer of light. He stared harder, and just made out a bundle of fur by the fireside, in the very same position as the previous night.

His heart pounded with delight. 'Thank goodness!' he chirped, feeling a tremendous sense of relief. He forced his gaze from Poohka to examine the rest of the room, and caught sight of Señora Bruja's bulbous body protruding from a chair that looked ready to collapse. Her head had fallen back, her mouth was wide open, and a stream of dribble cascaded down onto her heaving chest.

Señor Buho's joy was short-lived. He realised that his problems were only just beginning.

'How on earth am I going to get Poohka out of there without waking the wicked witch?' he said out loud.

'With great difficulty,' replied a little mouse who was passing below. 'Nothing comes out alive apart from the old woman herself.' The mouse shuddered, then continued on her way.

Señor Buho felt hungry at the sight of the little mouse, but this was neither the time nor the place to indulge such a thought. This little mouse had been very brave to respond to Señor Buho.

'Wait – can you help me?' Señor Buho asked.

The mouse stopped and swung her head back. 'I don't think so,' she replied. 'I have been trying to find my mother – she was caught in one of the wicked witch's traps a few days ago.' As she spoke, a teardrop fell from her right eye.

'Well, maybe we could help each other. If we could get inside we could save them both,' said Señor Buho, thinking quickly.

'Oh, thank you, sir!' the little mouse cried. 'I will help as best I can, but I am only little.'

'Between the two of us we may be able to work something out,' he chirped. 'And call me Señor Buho.' It was the first time in his life he'd ever felt sorry for a mouse. 'What's your name, little mouse?'

'Señorita Raton,' replied the mouse shyly.

'Follow my lead, Señorita Raton, and be ready to take cover,' continued Señor Buho. 'I am going to tap on the window to see how deeply Señora Bruja is sleeping. If she stirs get ready to escape and hide.'

'I am ready when you are, Señor Buho!'

The owl rapped hard on the window, 'rat-a-tat-tat, rat-a-tat-tat, rat-a-tat-tat! At first there was no response from inside. Was she so deeply asleep they could go in without her noticing?

Señor Buho peered closer to the window. He saw the old witch's hand lift from her stomach and move towards her face.

'Oh no,' he said.

'What is it?' replied Señorita Raton anxiously.

'I think we've woken the horrible witch after all. Be prepared to hide if I give the signal.'

Señorita Raton did not make a squeak – she was shaking so violently she could not utter a word.

Señora Bruja raised her hand to her long extended nose and gave it a quick scratch before dropping it heavily back onto her bulging stomach. A few 'tut, tut, tuts' emerged from her saliva-filled mouth, followed by an even heavier rendition of snores.

This was the opportunity that Señor Buho had hoped for. He let out a sigh of relief and signalled for Señorita Raton to get closer to the front door.

'See if you can gently push open the door,' he instructed.

Señorita Raton approached the door cautiously and pushed, then pulled, with all her might. However nothing budged. Then Señor Buho flew to the door handle to release the catch. But it was no good. The door was firmly locked.

'Let's see if you can get through a gap in the door, to release the catch from the inside,' Señor Buho suggested.

Señorita Raton shook more violently than ever. 'I think it is too dangerous,' the little mouse replied quietly.

'You are a very brave mouse,' said Señor Buho. 'Think of your mother, who may be waiting for your help inside.'

Señor Buho did not like to tell Señorita Raton he had seen no sign of her mother inside the room. However, that wasn't to say she wasn't there, obscured by the dirty, dust-covered window. There was always the possibility she was still alive. Now was not the time to put doubt into the little mouse's head.

Without hesitating, Señorita Raton squeezed her body through a small gap near the hinge of the wooden door. Señor Buho waited patiently by the door handle.

'What's keeping you?' whispered Señor Buho after a few minutes.

'The door is kept locked with string. I have to break it to get it open.'

'Chew it with your teeth – that should do the job!' insisted Señor Buho. He wondered why he was always the one who had to come up with the ideas.

After a few more moments, Señor Buho heard a crash and a thump, and then the door was pushed open and Señorita Raton ran out.

'What on earth was all that racket about?' asked Señor Buho.

'The peg holding the door dropped as I bit through the string and it crashed onto the floor before I could stop it,' she panted. 'Then I fell too!'

'Did it wake the wicked witch?' demanded Señor Buho.

'I don't know, I didn't have time to look,' replied the mouse, her eyes welling up with tears.

Señor Buho flew back to what was left of the window ledge. To his amazement Señora Bruja was still sound asleep.

'Good news, little one,' he said, returning to the door. 'The wicked witch has not stirred. This means we can continue our rescue attempt!'

Señorita Raton stopped shaking quite as much. 'Let's get on with it, then!' she said.

Together, using Señor Buho's beak and talons, as well as Señorita Raton's legs, they managed to pull the door open just enough for Señor Buho to get inside the hut.

Señor Buho lifted his wing to cover his beak from the terrible, overwhelming smells. This was no place for anyone to live.

Señor Buho made his way over to Poohka, beckoning the little mouse to follow with a wing.

Señorita Raton came to a sudden halt and let out a high-pitched squeak. 'EEEEEEKKKKKK!'

'Shhhhhh!' hissed Señor Buho, terrified Señora Bruja would wake up.

Her chair began swaying and creaking loudly. 'Anytime now that chair is going to collapse. Then the wicked witch will surely wake up and we will all perish.'

'But Poohka's... a cat!' Señorita Raton stuttered, trembling again as she tumbled closer to the fireplace. 'You didn't tell me that! Anyway, I must look for my mother.' The little mouse ran across the floor in the other direction.

Señor Buho flew over to Señorita Raton, who hadn't got far. 'I will fly around to look for your mother – I have a better chance of finding her than you do. Go and see if you can wake Poohka.'

So the little mouse tiptoed in the direction of Poohka, her face frozen with terror. She prodded Poohka lightly on the nose, then pulled at each one of his whiskers in turn. Poohka didn't stir so Señorita Raton moved around to tug his tail instead.

'Keep going,' called Señor Buho from the other side of the room.

'But what if he wakes up and eats me?' Señorita Raton cried. But she continued anyway, biting the tip of Poohka's tail, very gently. Poohka was still fast asleep and breathing heavily.

Over by the broken sink, Señor Buho saw a rusty trap lying carelessly on the dirty work surface. There was no sign of Señorita Raton's mother but he continued to search for the sake of the little mouse.

Señor Buho landed next to the chopping board which was covered in dried blood.

'Oh dear,' he thought to himself, 'this is not looking promising.' Then he saw it, sticking out from the edge of a filthy tea towel. A small rigid tail that could only have belonged to one animal – a poor mouse! Señor Buho felt a pang in his heart. How was he going to tell this brave little mouse that her mother was gone!

Señor Buho composed himself, then flew down to Poohka's side. 'Still nothing?' he asked.

Señorita Raton shook her little furry head.

Señor Buho bent down and pecked with his beak a couple of times on Poohka's ears. Still nothing.

'Time for Plan B. We'll have to drag him out,' Señor Buho announced.

'Wait – did you find my mother?' the little mouse asked.

'There's no sign of her in here, but she may have escaped.' Señor Buho felt guilty for not being honest, but this was no place to tell Señorita Raton the truth.

The unlikely duo began to drag Poohka across the floor and quickly realised a Plan C was needed. Poohka was far too heavy to be pulled across the floor by an owl and a mouse. The only problem was, Señor Buho didn't have a Plan C!

Chapter 9 - The lightning storm

'Where am I?' said Poohka in a very drowsy voice. 'And who's that?'

'Thank goodness!' cried the familiar face of Señor Buho. 'We were just wondering what on earth to do with you. Now hurry – try to get up onto your feet. This is Señorita Raton but there is no time for any more questions – just do as I say,' the wise owl ordered.

As soon as Poohka struggled to lift himself he felt intense pain in his broken leg. He swayed then stumbled. Señorita Raton, a mouse with a very shaky disposition, watched on from a distance.

'Follow me,' said Señor Buho quietly, 'and whatever you do, do not wake the wicked witch.'

Poohka's vision was very hazy and he had trouble getting his balance. What was happening? His head was spinning and his legs were like jelly, but he tried to obey Señor Buho.

Eventually the three animals made it to the door and out into the fresh air of the forest.

'I must sleep,' murmured Poohka. 'I am so, so tired – please let me sleep.'

'Not now,' said Señor Buho. 'We must get you far away from this evil place, before Señora Bruja knows you are gone.'

An almighty crash from inside the dwelling made Poohka jump and stare back at the house.

'It's the wicked witch,' said Señorita Raton. 'She's woken up!'

'Wicked?' said Poohka. 'What do you mean?' Señor Bruja's loud cries and shouting were causing the whole house to vibrate. As quickly as they could, Señor Buho and Señorita Raton pushed Poohka towards the trees at the side of the building.

'Poohka, Señora Bruja is a terrible, evil witch,' Señor Buho explained. 'Goodness knows what she was planning for you. You must hide in the undergrowth and pray she does not find you.' The owl was already taking flight. 'Little one, stay in hiding until the coast is clear and I will return for you soon.'

Señorita Raton had already disappeared, so Poohka limped over towards the trees Señor Buho had pointed out. Once there he trembled, curled up in the undergrowth and listened to Señora Bruja's screams.

'Where are you, kitty, kitty, kitty?' Another crash, another thump.

'Nice kitty, kitty, kitty, come to me. I will feed you some more delicious rabbit stew.' Poohka suddenly realised what Señor Buho meant. Señora Bruja was planning to eat him!

With the faint light reflecting from the fire, Poohka could see her silhouette as she stood in the doorway with the scythe. He prayed with all his might the wicked witch would not come out into the forest to look for him.

Poohka kept as still as a statue, worried that Señora Bruja would hear any movement. He breathed shallowly, his breath misting in front of his face. Finally, Señora Bruja seemed to give up.

'I must put myself to bed,' she grumbled to herself as she bent double in the doorway. 'That rabbit stew must have been off!' She staggered away in the direction of her filthy, unmade bed. 'That cat cannot have gone far with his broken leg. I will find him for sure in the morning.'

'Not if I can help it!' thought Poohka. He wondered when Señor Buho would be back to collect him – there were still many hours of darkness left.

As he waited, Poohka dozed on and off, but his head felt fuzzy and he was worried that Señora Bruja would recover and come to find him in the forest.

At last, he heard the welcome sound of flapping wings.

'Poohka, Poohka, wake up! This is no time to sleep. We must make tracks right away,' bleeted Señor Buho.

Señorita Raton suddenly appeared from behind a tree. 'Señor Buho, I cannot find my mother anywhere,' she said sadly.

'Little one, come here and sit down,' Señor Buho said gently. 'I am afraid I may have some sad news for you.'

'The horrible witch has killed her, hasn't she?' the little mouse said, her voice cracking with distress.

'Sadly, I think you're right. You see, I found the tail of a mouse, with its tip missing, during my search,' he replied.

'That's her! Oh no! My mother lost the tip of her tail in a trap many months ago.'

Poohka didn't know what to do as he watched the sad mouse weep uncontrollably.

'Señorita Raton, listen to me,' said the wise owl. 'You must get yourself away from these woods, for no one is safe here. Poohka and I will continue on to the village side of the forest as soon as we can. Hopefully I can help Poohka get back to his home in Sotogrande without any further incidents.'

Señorita Raton nodded, and tears fell to the ground. 'I will accompany you to the edge of the forest, then I will try to start a new life in the village beyond. There's nothing to keep me here now that I have no family left,' replied Señorita Raton.

'Then we must all get going as quickly as we can,' said Señor Buho. 'Come on, Poohka, we must be on our way – the wicked witch could appear at any time.'

But these words were a blur to Poohka, who'd dozed back into a deep sleep. That is until Señorita Raton began nibbling at Poohka's tail and Señor Buho started pecking away at his ears.

Poohka woke abruptly and gave a start. His ears were now hurting, his tail was sore and his broken leg was throbbing badly. 'What – what is it?' asked Poohka, perplexed. He looked up to see Señor Buho staring down at him with an air of superiority.

'Come on, Poohka, we must go now, before you get us into any more trouble,' Señor Buho demanded. 'We only have a couple of hours before it gets light and Señora Bruja will definitely be on the warpath by then. We must move fast, so get on your feet. From now on, no matter what else you do, do not befriend anyone other than Señorita Raton and myself. It's too dangerous!'

With his head bowed, Poohka lifted his painful body to stand up. Despite his great tiredness, he managed to hobble his way through the undergrowth until they were all some distance from the wicked witch and her house.

As they journeyed through the forest, Señor Buho explained that Señorita Raton's mother had been eaten by the wicked witch, and that Poohka himself, he guessed, was to be her next supply of food. Poohka realised how lucky he was to have escaped, and all thanks to Señor Buho and Señorita Raton. He owed them his life.

Just before the sun started to rise, Señor Buho flew down close to Poohka. 'Adios, I must depart now, but I will return once more at nightfall. I expect you to continue on your journey during daylight hours.'

Poohka nodded – he knew he had to keep going now that the tiredness of earlier was wearing off.

Señor Buho flapped away and called out, 'We're nearly at the edge of the forest – follow this road out. Keep off the pavement, but stay close by in the undergrowth. And keep out of sight at all times. I will meet you at the entrance to the white village. You won't be able to miss it – it's at the bottom of the steep hill.'

Poohka and Señorita Raton waved to the owl.

Señor Buho circled above them. 'We will continue once more when darkness falls. Until then, be safe, my friends!' Then he was gone from sight, and Poohka was left alone with Señorita Raton.

The little mouse was still sniffling and holding back her tears. Poohka, meanwhile, dropped his body to the ground, exhausted by the journey to the edge of the forest.

'I do not think we can stop here, Poohka,' sniffed Señorita Raton. 'It will not take the horrible Señora Bruja long to find us – we must continue to the village, then we can both rest.'

The sun was just starting to rise, but there was a heaviness in the air, and everything around was very still. The forest was eerily silent save for the howl of a wolf in the distance, sending alarm signals to the other creatures in the forest.

'Come on then, Señorita, let us make our way to the village for safety. Maybe we will find food and shelter there,' Poohka replied. 'But I feel something strange in the air. We must make haste.'

The journey in the undergrowth parallel to the road seemed long and arduous. It would have been easier to travel on the pavement but Poohka knew this would be far too dangerous. At least the sun was not beating down, but dark clouds had begun to appear above. There was no sound of bird song, only the roar of cars passing by on the road at speed. The air began to feel heavier.

'It feels as if we're going to have a storm,' Poohka decided as he limped uncomfortably towards the village in the distance. He could see it waiting for him at the bottom of a long, steep hill.

Seconds after Poohka spoke, the sky lit up and a fork of lightning shot down, followed quickly by an almighty clap of thunder from above.

'What was that?' trembled Señorita Raton who was some way ahead of Poohka. She'd been making her way by darting in-between the dried hedgerow and discarded rubbish. She was young, and Poohka guessed she'd never seen a storm before.

Poohka knew storms only too well. 'Thunder and lightning,' the cat replied. 'We better find some shelter.' He pointed ahead. 'I can see some rubbish carts up there – we can protect ourselves beneath them for the time being.'

They made their way to the rubbish carts as quickly as they could.

By the time they arrived at the overflowing carts, the storm was in full force. The lightning was striking frequently, followed almost immediately by large claps of thunder. Just as they reached the bins, the heavens opened and the rain began to fall heavily.

'Quick, get under here,' Poohka instructed as he slid under the largest of the rubbish containers on wheels.

They were both already drenched by the sudden downpour of rain. It had soaked everything around them in moments. As the pair waited for the storm to pass, they shook their bodies to remove the excess water from their coats. Señorita Raton was trembling violently now.

'We will rest here for a while. Come, curl up in my fur and keep warm,' Poohka offered. He felt sorry for the small orphaned mouse.

Poohka could see the fear on Señorita Raton's face. She was clearly terrified of him. 'I will not harm you, little one,' he reassured her. 'You helped to save my life, so it is the least I can do for you.'

Señorita Raton moved slowly towards Poohka, cautiously curling up around his tummy area. Eventually, Poohka could feel her shakes subside and her breathing steady. Later, as the rain continued to pour down, the little mouse finally fell into a deep sleep.

Poohka watched over the little mouse as she slept buried in his fur. Thankfully they were safe here from the torrential rain, thunder and lightning. Poohka was exhausted too, and before he knew it, he'd fallen asleep. Each thunder and lightning strike jolted his eyes open for a moment, but he quickly returned to his slumber.

The little mouse snuggled deeper into Poohka's fur. Poohka stirred a little as the storm subsided. The rains continued, but he didn't mind. Yes, it was hindering their journey but he realised what else it meant and was suddenly filled with an overwhelming sense of happiness. These rains would save kind Señor Arbol back at the landfill site!

Chapter 10 - A home for a mouse

Poohka felt a gentle tongue cleaning his face. It was so gentle it reminded him of his dear mother, when she had washed and kept him safe as a kitten. It was a wonderful sensation and Poohka was not sure whether it was a dream or for real. He did not want to open his eyes in case it stopped. The softness of the tongue on his head gave him a sense of well-being. It warmed his heart, and gave him hope, and eventually he couldn't help but open his eyes.

It was not a dream, nor was it his mother's tongue but Poohka's heart melted as he looked up at the most beautiful cat he had ever seen. Her magnetic blue eyes looked down at him with concern while the mystery feline continued to wash every inch of Poohka's face and neck. Poohka felt a tingling sensation throughout his body.

With his eyes closed once more, enjoying every second of this tender wash, Poohka felt the movement of Señorita Raton within his fur. This brought Poohka immediately to his senses, as he became concerned for the safety of the little mouse. But he wouldn't stop the gentle washing; not yet – it was too good.

Eventually Poohka broke the silence. 'Who are you?' he muttered, realising immediately that these were not the words he wanted to say (how rude he must have sounded!). Poohka was so confused – one minute he was sheltering underneath the rubbish skips from the torrential rain and the next he was being cleaned by the most stunning cat he had ever seen. Poohka tried to pull himself together and fumbled for words. 'Oh... Sorry... I... I... I thought I was dreaming. Thank you for cleaning me up. My name is Poohka. I am delighted to meet you. Thank you,' he said again, this time with a little more composure.

'That's OK,' purred the beautiful cat. 'My name is Pequita. I came here to shelter from the storm. I have been here for a few hours. You have been in a deep, deep sleep. I cleaned you up as you were very muddy. It looks like you've been in the wars.'

Poohka nodded wordlessly.

'I hope you don't mind,' she continued. 'Once the rains ease off I must hurry on my way to my family. This is not a safe place to be.'

'Oh, must you go?' Poohka managed.

'Yes, I must,' replied Pequita without hesitation, 'and so must you. When nightfall comes, this is the hideout for a gang of giant rats living in this area. They will not take kindly to you being here. They take no prisoners.' Pequita shuddered as if to emphasize her words.

'You're obviously not a local,' she said. 'Otherwise you would not have been sleeping so deeply in such a dangerous place.'

Poohka felt a small paw tapping frantically at his stomach. He realised he had forgotten all about Señorita Raton.

'Uh-oh,' Poohka thought. 'What am I to do?'

Poohka, worried about how he could protect little Señorita Raton from becoming a meal for Pequita, gently pushed Señorita Raton further into his fur. He needed time to think. Looking at Pequita, Poohka felt sure her life was not easy. She probably had to scavenge for her food to look after her family. This was going to be very difficult. Pequita would surely pounce on Señorita Raton if she caught sight of the little mouse. Poohka decided he would have to explain to Pequita how Señorita Raton saved his life and beg her to resist the temptation of killing the mouse to feed her family. Poohka trembled at the thought – he was not sure exactly how Pequita would respond. He had only just met the beautiful feline – there was no knowing what she would do!

'The rains are easing off now. We must leave this dangerous spot before it gets dark. I can show you a safe place where you can take shelter,' Pequita offered, interrupting Poohka's thoughts.

'Oh, oh, yes, thank you,' Poohka stammered. 'But, Pequita, before we move from here, I have something I must tell you. I am not alone,' Poohka lowered his voice to a whisper. 'I have a friend with me who saved my life in the forest.'

'I think you must be very much mistaken,' replied Pequita, laughing. 'There is no one else here – just the two of us.'

'I am afraid you are wrong,' Poohka continued. 'But I need you to promise me you will not do anything to harm my friend.'

'Well, that depends on who it is!' said Pequita.

'Please promise me you will not attack or harm Señorita Raton. She really is an amazingly brave mouse.' There, he had said it and now he froze, wondering what would happen next.

Pequita began to giggle, then her laughter became uncontrollable – she rolled over and over in fits of giggles. When she eventually composed herself, she still found it hard to reply to Poohka without giggling her response. 'You mean a mouse...' chuckle... chuckle... '...saved your life...?' chuckle... chuckle... 'You cannot be serious!' Her uncontrollable laughter continued.

This display of hysteria did not instil any confidence in Poohka. In fact he was even more concerned for the welfare of little Señorita Raton now that he had let the cat out of the bag! He pushed out his hind leg to wedge Señorita Raton deeper into his fur for added protection.

Eventually, after many more chuckles and giggles, Pequita collapsed and closed both eyes. 'OK then, show me your friend!'

Señorita Raton made no attempt to move from deep within Poohka's fur – and Poohka wasn't surprised. He could feel her trembling in fear.

Poohka gently nuzzled his nose into his own fur, close to where Señorita Raton was hiding. Very slowly, Señorita Raton emerged from the safety of Poohka's coat, keeping as close to him as she could, ready to dive back under Poohka if it was necessary. Poohka remained alert, knowing he would have to go on the defensive if Pequita showed any signs of aggression.

'Well, I have never in all of my life seen anything like this before!' Pequita said. 'How on earth did this little mouse save your life?'

'It is a long story,' replied Poohka, sensing the worst was over. Señorita Raton seemed safe for the time being.

'Well, we do not have time for long stories. We must get out of here straightaway! You will have to tell me later.'

'But what about Señorita Raton? I cannot leave her here, all alone,' sighed Poohka sadly.

Pequita had begun to walk away, but turned to look at the little mouse once again. 'She must come with us,' she decided. 'I will take you to the mouse colony where she can join the other mice in the village, but I cannot vouch for her safety once she is there. We are all fighting for survival here, and whilst I may respect your wishes, Poohka, others will not. Once she is with the mouse colony they will take care of her. It is the safest place for her, and it is the best I can do.'

Pequita spun back round again. 'Now we must be on our way, before the rats arrive! Otherwise we will all be in danger.'

Pequita darted off in the direction of the village. With some relief, Poohka and Señorita Raton followed along at a much slower pace – Poohka's leg slowed him down and the little mouse stayed very close to the ginger and white cat for protection.

They hadn't gone far when, once more, the heavens opened and the rain fell. When they eventually caught up with Pequita, she was sheltering from the downpour under a table outside the local tapas bar. Pequita pointed a paw in the direction of the empty building next door, explaining, 'This is where the mouse colony lives. Señorita Raton will be safe there.'

Señorita Raton looked up at Poohka with tears in her eyes. She rubbed close to his body and said, 'Farewell, Poohka, I hope you find your way to Sotogrande and your broken leg is fixed soon.'

'I will return to this spot in the morning to check you are OK, dear friend,' Poohka said softly, as he cuddled the little mouse. 'I hope you will be happy in your new home, far away from Señora Bruja.'

'Until tomorrow morning,' replied Señorita Raton.

Pequita and Poohka watched and smiled as Señorita Raton ran cautiously towards the broken front door, into the gloomy dark building, and disappeared.

Chapter 11 - The beautiful Pequita

Pequita was already hurrying up the cobbled road, taking cover every now and again from the rain under a variety of chairs and tables.

Poohka struggled to keep up now; his leg was hurting so much. But he had to try. He had to stay focused for fear of losing sight of Pequita.

After a time, Pequita finally slowed down and waited for Poohka to reach her before continuing up the winding, steep cobbled road. Had she realised how bad Poohka's injury really was?

'Not long now, Poohka, and we will be at my humble home,' called Pequita.

'I am sorry to delay you, and to be causing you so much trouble,' Poohka replied.

Pequita ignored Poohka's apology. 'I want you to meet my family. I think you will like them. They are a lively little lot, but we have lots of fun and laughter in our household.'

Just then they arrived at the front of a charming home with pretty flower baskets hanging outside the wooden front door. By the side of the door a few bricks were missing which left a hole big enough for a cat to enter. Pequita climbed in, followed closely by Poohka.

Once they'd reached the other side, Poohka had to do a double-take. In front of him was a beautiful garden, leading to another inner front door. To the left of this were steps which led down to an empty room beneath the property.

As they climbed down the steps, Poohka walking carefully on three legs, Pequita smiled and said, 'Welcome to my home, Poohka.'

Although it was a small room, stacked up with outdoor garden furniture, in a corner of the tiled floor were two baby mattresses. Blankets were neatly placed on top.

On entering the room, five little heads lifted from the furthest mattress, and all of a sudden the kittens came rushing at full speed to their adoring mother.

'Hey, hey, hold on a minute, little ones, you will knock me over if you aren't careful!' exclaimed Pequita.

The kittens playfully tussled with one another and jumped up at their mother, seeking her attention.

'Calm down, all of you – we have a visitor! I would like you to meet Poohka,' Pequita said with a purr.

Poohka realised that he was not a pretty sight. They'd been caught in the torrential rain and were now both trembling with the chill of their wet fur. He was glad of the shelter and warmth Pequita's home could offer him.

The kittens were clearly all so delighted to have Pequita safely back at home that they found it hard not to show their emotions. They licked at her frantically to dry her soaking fur.

Eventually they moved forward cautiously towards Poohka who was still standing, drenched to the skin, with his broken paw lifted off the ground. One by one, they approached timidly, but as their mother spoke again, they rushed straight back to her.

'Poohka, come over here – keep warm and get dry,' Pequita insisted. 'I hope that soon the elderly lady who lives above will bring leftovers down for us. We are most fortunate here – the lady is kind. She gives us food from time to time. It is not much, but it helps to keep my family going.'

Poohka moved closer to the cosy looking mattress. He had never slept on a proper bed before, and it looked so inviting. The kittens were now more interested in the unknown visitor and less nervous. They climbed up to join Poohka and began to check him over inquisitively.

Pequita moved forward and curled up with Poohka, giving warmth to his trembling body. Poohka felt his heart melt in this wonderful, caring environment. He felt at home, and all his troubles seemed to melt away – until one of the kittens decided to jump on top of him, right onto his broken leg.

Poohka let out a yell, and all five of the kittens went scurrying to the other mattress beyond their mother's reach or scolding.

But the pain subsided quickly, and Poohka soon closed his eyes and drifted off to sleep, the warmth of Pequita's body close to his.

Poohka was woken by one of the kittens nuzzling close to his head and purring. He could not begin to describe how contented he felt at that very moment. If it weren't for his injury and the pain it caused him, this would be perfect and he would never want to leave.

All of a sudden there were footsteps on the concrete steps outside the door. The kittens' ears pricked up and they scampered towards the doorway. An elderly, heavily built lady emerged; holding onto the door handle to steady herself, she puffed with exhaustion.

'Here we are, little kittens. I have some meats and cheese for you to fill your stomachs,' the lady said in a weak, shaky voice. She placed the container on the floor then turned to exit the room, but suddenly stopped and looked down again – right at Poohka.

'I cannot take on any more hungry cats,' she puffed. 'You will have to share the food with the others, then you must be gone. There is no room for any more.' She began climbing the steps awkwardly, returning to her home above.

'I must go,' said Poohka. 'The lady does not want me here.'

'No, you must stay,' insisted Pequita. 'You are in no state to go anywhere. The lady will come round in time, I am sure. Anyway, for now you must have something to eat. The kittens have eaten all the cheese, but thankfully they do not like meat yet.'

The two ate the chunks of meat in silence, and Poohka soon felt wonderfully satisfied, especially now he was dry from the warmth of the room. He could still hear the storm continuing outside, but Poohka was content in the knowledge he was safe in this comfortable place with the beautiful Pequita.

When darkness fell, Poohka was allocated one of the mattresses to ensure he had a good night's sleep. But once he had fallen into a deep sleep, Pequita freed herself from her kittens and padded quietly over to curl up close to Poohka. Through the night the kittens came to join them, one by one, until they were all fast asleep on Poohka's mattress.

Poohka opened his eyes as the early morning light entered the room. 'I feel as though I am part of a very happy family – how wonderful!' Poohka thought to himself as he looked around at Pequita and her little ones all curled up asleep with him. A ripping pain suddenly rushed through his broken leg as one of the little ones' legs stretched out. It reminded Poohka of his injury and that he really should have it seen to.

Thoughts started running through Poohka's mind: 'Could I stay here forever with Pequita and her family? Would the lady above allow me to stay, and would she help me with my broken leg? Or should I return to my friends in Sotogrande where there is more chance of my leg being fixed, and where I could continue life there with my friends?' The questions kept coming, hurtling through his brain. Poohka did not know what to do.

The rains continued outside, but Poohka knew he had to go down to the tapas bar to check on Señorita Raton. He had promised he would return, and he hoped the little mouse would be happy in her new home.

The kittens started to stir, so Poohka took the opportunity to lift himself carefully onto his three good legs. He slowly made his way to the open doorway, indicating to the kittens to keep quiet so their mother could rest a little more.

'I will return soon,' Poohka whispered to the kittens. 'Let your mother sleep and please behave yourselves.' He climbed the stairs cautiously but also with a lot of difficulty, and went into the rain outside.

Poohka got his bearings and slowly made his way down the quiet cobbled road. He was headed for the tapas bar at the bottom of the hill.

The rain poured down. Even before he reached the corner of the road he was drenched to the skin, but he didn't let that stop him, even as he skidded on the slippery cobbled surface. Thankfully no one was around to see him.

Suddenly there was a large crack of thunder, and Poohka's heart leapt and missed a couple of beats. Before he knew it, he'd slipped on the wet cobbles and fallen face down into the gully that divided the pathway with the cobbled road. At that moment, a car passed in a rush and sprayed the water covering the road to each side of the vehicle, drenching anything in its path.

Poohka was now completely submerged and gasping for breath. The tyres of the car had missed him by millimetres and his heart pounded so hard he thought it was about to burst. What's more, people were starting to appear on the streets, rushing to get to their destination. The activity worried Poohka, as it meant he could no longer travel unnoticed.

Now, more than ever, he wanted to get back to the tranquillity and protection of Pequita's house or his lovely home in Sotogrande. As he climbed tentatively out of the gully, he knew that, one way or another, he had to regain his strength and get straight down to the tapas bar as quickly as he could. At least there he'd be able to shelter from the storm overhead.

Finally, after what seemed like a much longer journey than before, he made it to the table positioned outside the tapas bar, where he was due to meet Señorita Raton. Poohka looked around at himself. He was soaking wet and covered in mud, no longer a handsome ginger and white cat.

As he stood waiting, despair overwhelmed him. 'How has one careless mistake brought me to such a terrible situation?' he thought sadly.

The rains were getting heavier, matching Poohka's dark mood, and he wondered if Señorita Raton would ever turn up. He kept a steady eye on the entrance next to the tapas bar, but there was no sign of life. Impatiently, Poohka spluttered a strange-sounding, 'Meow', his mouth still containing some of the dirty water from the puddle he'd fallen into.

Señorita Raton was fast asleep after a long night relating the adventures she had experienced with Poohka – how she had ended up being friends with a cat. Now, most of the mice looked up to her, although some of the older ones weren't convinced by her story.

Señorita Raton did not hear Poohka's pathetic meow, but one of the elders did. As was their drill, he quickly sent out an alert to signal that the enemy was in close proximity. It was this squealing alert that woke Señorita Raton and at first she did not know where she was. She had been in a very deep sleep.

She nudged the little mouse next to her who was already wide awake and waiting for orders.

'What's going on?' enquired Señorita Raton.

'There is a cat in the vicinity! We must all be ready to evacuate the building if necessary,' the mouse explained.

'What time is it?' asked Señorita Raton.

'Don't worry about the time,' said the anxious mouse, 'just be prepared to move off as quickly as you can should the cat venture any closer to the building.'

'But I need to know what time of day it is,' persisted Señorita Raton.

'It's morning-time, silly,' replied the annoyed mouse.

Señorita Raton sat up like a shot and boldly walked to the doorway, peering outside.

'Come back, come back!' cried the other mice. 'There's a cat outside!'

Chapter 12 - A home from home

At first Señorita Raton did not recognise Poohka. He was drenched to the skin and his beautiful ginger and white coat was grey and muddy, but she knew no other cat would venture out in this terrible weather, however hungry they were, and with an injured leg.

Señorita Raton scurried out in the torrential rain to join Poohka, taking shelter under the table on the pavement.

'Oh, Poohka, where have you been?' Señorita Raton said. 'You look terrible!'

'I have had better days, but I have been well looked after – although it may not look like it,' Poohka replied with a shiver and a weary smile.

Out of the corner of his eye, Poohka could see all of the mice in the derelict building come slowly to the doorway to see where Señorita Raton had run off to in such a hurry.

'Is this the right place for you to live?' asked Poohka, happy to see Señorita Raton looking so content.

'Poohka, you must not be concerned about me,' said Señorita Raton, beaming. 'I will be very happy here, and I know I will make lots of friends. What's important is that you need to build your strength until the rains pass. Then Señor Buho will return to lead you on your way – back to Sotogrande, back to your home.'

Señorita Raton turned and glanced at the entire mouse commune looking at her through the doorway in astonishment.

'Farewell, Poohka,' she said boldly. 'Have a safe journey to Sotogrande. Good luck!'

Poohka felt so relieved Señorita Raton would be happy living here. 'Thank you, Señorita Raton, for saving my life. I shall never forget you,' he said as the little mouse ran back to the broken doorway, playfully avoiding the puddles on the pavement as she went.

The mice all quickly disappeared inside, but Poohka waited until the rains eased a little before he turned and cautiously made his way back up the cobbled road.

On his way, he felt a sudden wave of shame. He had not thought of Señor Buho who would also be affected by the heavy rains. Poohka realised that at nightfall he must make his way down to the entrance of the village to wait for the owl to arrive, even if it was just to say he would not require his assistance anymore. He owed Señor Buho that much.

By the time he was back at the entrance to Pequita's doorway, the sun was trying to shine from behind a cloud. He felt sure this was going to be a lovely day after all.

As Poohka descended the steps, he heard movement from within. At first the little kittens darted behind their mother. Poohka was surprised, and then realised what was wrong – they did not recognise this dirty, muddy cat descending with difficulty down the steps.

'Don't be silly, little ones, it's only Poohka,' Pequita reassured them. 'I was worried about you – look at the state you are in. Where on earth have you been?' Pequita asked tenderly. 'Come over here and I will clean you up.'

Before long Poohka was looking more like himself and feeling a lot happier. He was warm and content in this wonderful home with the beautiful, caring Pequita.

The kittens were playing close by and coming over every now and again to check Poohka was properly cleaned, giving him a lick as they did so.

Poohka explained where he had been and how he had become so wet and dirty. He related his meeting with Señorita Raton and how he was content in the knowledge she would be happy living here in the village with the mouse commune.

They spent a restful day with the sun bursting through the doorway. Poohka felt the most relaxed he had felt since his fateful day at the rubbish tip. He could happily stay here, being well taken care of by the gorgeous Pequita, with her cute kittens running around between them.

Poohka's bad leg had now been thoroughly cleaned. Pequita had done her best with the wound to make it more comfortable for him. Still, whenever he moved, sharp jolts of pain shot through it, and though he tried not to show it, Pequita could tell how painful it was for him. Poohka really needed proper treatment, and this was something she couldn't give him.

Poohka's leg became more painful throughout the day. He tried to doze, but it was difficult to sleep. Later, Pequita positioned herself away from Poohka's bad leg and placed her head gently on his tummy. She drifted off into a contented sleep. Poohka could tell she wanted to do more to help him, but a broken leg couldn't be fixed with licks and care alone.

Poohka opened his eyes slightly and looked down at Pequita. He wanted to enjoy this moment. She was such a kind and gentle soul; he could happily stay here like this forever.

When Pequita stirred, Poohka didn't take his eyes away from her. After a few moments she whispered, 'Poohka, why not stay here with us? You do not need to go all the way to Sotogrande. I will look after you.'

Maybe his leg would fix itself in time if he stayed here. But Poohka had another thought. 'What about the lady upstairs? She did not take kindly to my being here.'

'I am sure she will come around in time,' Pequita insisted.

Poohka had decided. He didn't want to leave. 'If I am to stay, I must tell Señor Buho of my intentions when I see him tonight.'

Pequita sat up. 'Who is Señor Buho, and why will you be telling him tonight of your change of plans?'

'Señor Buho has guided me on my journey so far. He was taking me back to Sotogrande,' Poohka explained. 'When Señor Buho left me at the edge of the forest, he said he would return for me at nightfall by the entrance to the village. With the storms and rains he has not yet returned, but now the storm has passed, he will be waiting for me tonight. I must be there to tell him I will no longer require his help now I have decided that I wish to stay here.' Poohka struggled to smile as his leg throbbed with pain.

'But why are you travelling with Señor Buho at night?' asked Pequita. 'Is it not safer for you to travel in daylight?'

'Señor Buho is an owl, so he can only travel at night,' Poohka explained.

'Oh, Poohka, you do surprise me with all your friends! Don't tell me he saved your life as well?' she asked.

'Well, yes, he did. I also owe him a debt of gratitude.' Poohka remembered all that Señor Buho had done for him so far.

'I am glad you have decided to stay,' Pequita whispered to Poohka as she glanced over to her kittens, who were sleeping peacefully in the heat of the day.

Time passed and early evening came. Poohka left the comfort of Pequita's home, slowly limping his way down to the entrance of the village. He found a small area of shrubs and bushes not far from the tapas bar where he could hide as he waited for nightfall and the arrival of Señor Buho.

Poohka sat patiently among the shrubs waiting for Señor Buho to appear. He started to worry. He knew Señor Buho would be cross with him for wasting his time, although he was sure he was making the right decision to stay here with Pequita and her little ones. He had fallen madly in love with her – he could not bear for them to be parted. Hopefully he could get his broken leg sorted out somehow and then everything would be perfect.

As evening gave way to night, Poohka became concerned. He hadn't seen or heard any sign of Señor Buho. But he would wait a little longer, in case Señor Buho had been delayed.

Poohka's eyes started to close, and he realised he had been waiting for some hours now. Surely it was too late for Señor Buho to come now. 'I should stay just a few minutes more in case Señor Buho has been delayed,' he thought. 'And then I will return to Pequita.'

Poohka's eyes became heavier and heavier. Eventually he gave in to sleep.

When Poohka awoke, he did not know how long he had been asleep. He was only aware of birdsong in the distance. It was nearly morning! There had been no sign of Señor Buho. He knew he'd have to return once again tonight to explain his intentions – if Señor Buho ever came back. For now it was time to return to his new-found love, Pequita.

'Where have you been?' exclaimed Pequita with concern as Poohka gingerly descended the steps. 'I have been so worried about you. I thought you had changed your mind about staying and you'd left without even saying goodbye.'

Having returned as fast as he could using only his three legs, Poohka stumbled into Pequita's home. His broken leg was now causing him so much pain, he just wanted to collapse on the mattress.

'I am sorry, Pequita. Señor Buho never turned up, and I fell asleep,' panted Poohka. 'I will have to return this evening to see if he comes for me tonight.' Poohka fell onto the unoccupied mattress. The kittens were still fast asleep, all curled up together on the other bed. Pequita moved next to Poohka, and gently began washing him. Within minutes he was fast asleep.

When Poohka opened his eyes, Pequita was there by his side, her eyes alight with encouragement. But he was beginning to wonder if it was right for him to depend on Pequita's goodwill and kindness – she had more than enough responsibilities of her own.

Poohka's mind was in a whirl again. Should he stay or should he go? But he was so tired he could not answer the question. He drifted back off to sleep.

Poohka was awoken by shouting and shot up, landing painfully on his broken leg yet again. 'We cannot take on any more cats, injured or not!' the old lady from upstairs was squealing, while Pequita stood frozen and her kittens hid in a corner. 'My husband is struggling as it is to pay the bills, and another mouth to feed is completely out of the question. Make sure that ginger cat's out of here by tomorrow, otherwise I will get my neighbour to take it away.'

Pequita sat trembling; she had never seen the old lady behave this way before. She rushed over to her kittens who were terrified in the corner, not knowing what to do. Once their mother was by their side, they all calmed down.

The old lady left the food basket on the floor and stormed up the steps, puffing and panting while clutching the handrail for support.

Poohka looked at Pequita, who was trembling. Once more the mother cat rushed over to her kittens to calm them down with licks and strokes.

But the old lady hadn't quite finished. 'You better be gone by tomorrow or else!' she yelled.

Chapter 13 - A difficult goodbye

Once they heard the front door slam, the kittens rushed over to the basket and, one by one, clambered inside. The scare with the old lady was quickly forgotten though, and they ate their food with enthusiasm. But for Poohka it was far from forgotten. Pequita went slowly over to him, her eyes wet with sadness. She licked Poohka's face, and he slowly began to relax a little, not knowing what to say or do.

Pequita was the first to speak. 'Poohka, everything will be all right, I'm sure of it. We will make sure you are not here when she comes down with the food each day. We can ration the food, and you can return here each night when the coast is clear,' she said reassuringly.

Poohka took a deep breath and let it out slowly. 'Pequita, you are the dearest, kindest cat I have ever met, but I do not think it will work,' he replied. 'If I get caught here again, goodness knows where I'll end up. What's more, the lady might decide to throw you all out, and then you'll be homeless and without food. I cannot let this happen to you all.'

Poohka was sad it had come to this, but he knew in his heart that his only chance of survival was to return to his home in Sotogrande, where he was sure someone would take care of him and help to mend his broken leg.

'Tonight I will return to the entrance of the village,' he continued. 'Hopefully Señor Buho will be there, and I will continue my journey.' Poohka sighed. 'I will miss you all so much, but I know I must go for everyone's sake.'

Pequita had tears in her eyes, but before they had a chance to fall, she rushed over to her kittens who were munching away in the basket. One by one she removed them, and Poohka wondered what she was doing. Then he realised – she wanted him to eat as much as possible before beginning his journey back to Sotogrande.

The kittens quickly forgot the food and began playing with one another, darting all over the place. Meanwhile, Poohka lowered his head and slowly began to eat. By the time he had finished eating, the kittens had stopped playing, exhausted. One by one they returned to the mattress where they curled up together in a loving heap. Contented, they fell asleep, unaware of the situation.

Just before the sun was about to set, Poohka began preparing himself for his journey. Pequita had insisted she accompany Poohka to the village entrance to see him safely on his way. Poohka said his silent goodbyes to the sleeping kittens as the two cats crept out of Pequita's home.

With heavy hearts they made their final trip together to the entrance of the village.

Pequita tried to keep Poohka's spirits up by chatting to him all the way. 'Poohka, when the kittens are grown up, maybe I could find my way to Sotogrande and join you there,' she said hopefully.

Though he knew it was unlikely ever to happen, Poohka responded with enthusiasm, so as not to dampen Pequita's spirits. 'I would like that very much, Pequita. You will always be welcome at my home in Sotogrande.'

Both Pequita and Poohka sat quietly by the lamppost as the night drew in. Poohka didn't dare say anything, fearful of upsetting Pequita further. It was going to be hard enough when the time came to say goodbye.

It seemed they had been waiting for a long time in the dark and Poohka realised he couldn't wait for ever. 'I will have to start my journey on my own,' he decided. 'Obviously something has happened to Señor Buho, and he can no longer assist me. I know I must head south, so I will continue until I reach the coast. I can find my way by the stars.' After surviving a long and arduous journey so far, Poohka felt sure he could somehow make it.

He stood up to say a final farewell to Pequita.

'I will miss you terribly, Pequita. I have never loved anyone as much as I love you. You will always be in my thoughts. Please take care of yourself and your little ones.' Poohka stopped to swallow a lump in his throat, then continued. 'If you ever make it to Sotogrande, I will be waiting for you. And so I will not say 'adios', only 'hasta luego'. Hopefully we will be together again one day.'

Pequita licked Poohka's face with tears in her eyes. Poohka understood that she was far too upset to speak.

Poohka turned slowly towards the south as tears fell from his eyes.

'Hasta luego, Poohka, take care, I will miss you!' Pequita called after Poohka, managing a few words of farewell at last.

Chapter 14 - A hard road to take

As Poohka wiped away his tears and focused on the road ahead, he heard a sharp squawk – and then another. 'Wait for me!' cried Señor Buho. 'Where do you think you are going without me?' he shrieked.

Poohka stopped in his tracks and gave a deep sigh of relief. He'd been willing to carry on his journey alone, but he was so happy to see Señor Buho he could have kissed him. Not that he'd let Señor Buho know this. 'Oh, it is good to see you, Señor Buho,' replied Poohka confidently. 'I thought something dreadful might have happened to you. I was waiting for you last night, but you didn't turn up.'

'What do you mean "didn't turn up"?' squawked Señor Buho. 'I was there. It was YOU who did not turn up. After hours of waiting, I finally did the journey alone, thinking you may have started without me. Of course I never found you. However,' Señor Buho seemed to soften, 'I have seen ahead and the good news is that you are nearing the end of your journey. You should be there by tomorrow if you keep a good pace and do not stop too often.'

Poohka could not believe it. He was nearly there!

'But there is also some bad news: it is road all the way, and it is dangerous. There are some maniacs on the road at night.'

'But, Señor Buho, I did turn up...' Poohka tried to explain, but the owl was paying no attention.

'Come on, there's no time to waste! Just keep going straight on this road,' Señor Buho called out as he flew into the distance above the road ahead.

Poohka tried to walk a little quicker, but his broken leg kept getting in his way. The pain intensified. Poohka kept telling himself there was only a day to go – just a few hours – so he must put up with the throbbing, shooting pains in his leg. Soon he would be at home in Sotogrande, where he desperately hoped someone would take care of his broken leg.

The road seemed long and steep. In parts the surface was broken up and bumpy, so walking was difficult. He had to keep to the road as it was surrounded by very rocky, rugged land, which was impossible to walk on.

Poohka could see lights in the distance. Before he knew it, cars were nearly on top of him.

'This is not going to be an easy part of my journey,' Poohka thought to himself.

Each time a car came he would move quickly into the rocky area to the side of the road to dodge the oncoming vehicles. But jumping down from the level of the road meant more pain and more time recovering before returning to the raised level of the old road.

'Please, please let me make it home safely,' Poohka prayed. 'I have come so far – please give me the strength to carry on.'

At that moment, Señor Buho flew back to Poohka. 'Stop mumbling to yourself. Get a move on,' he scolded. 'At this rate it will take you a week to get back and there is no safe place to shelter here from the heat of the day. Not to mention that the road will become much busier.'

'But my leg is so painful. I am having trouble...' Poohka's voice disappeared into the distance, as once more Señor Buho flew off ahead.

To raise his spirits, Poohka started thinking of all the happy things back in Sotogrande – listening to 3jabs's stories, walking with Alex and Annabel. It made him smile just to think about them – and how close he was to returning. But as the road became busier his thoughts distracted him, and he realised he needed to keep his wits about him. There would be time for thinking later – once he was back. The road was starting to bend more often, and Poohka was struggling to continue up the hill. It became difficult to see oncoming vehicles – several times a car would be upon him suddenly, and Poohka would slip into the gully at the side.

Then Poohka felt a shooting pain rip through his body – everything had happened so fast. One minute he was on the winding road keeping close to the curb just before a bend, when all of a sudden he was dazzled by the headlights ahead. He froze for only a couple of seconds because of the lights, but that was all it took. Poohka felt the side of the front bumper brush his broken leg. The next thing he knew he had tumbled down between the rocks in the gully of the road. Crash! Then there was nothing, just blackness...

Poohka felt dizzy and sick. How long had he been in the gully? And how would he get out? Then he heard a familiar voice.

'Poohka... Poohka... Poohka, can you hear me? Are you all right? Please give me a sign you are still alive,' called Señor Buho.

Señor Buho couldn't see him! Poohka drew in a long breath and managed a sudden, piercing 'Meeoowww' that echoed around the rocky area. 'My leg hurts so much!' Poohka cried.

'Thank goodness you're alive!' Poohka was relieved to see Señor Buho's head peek down in to the gully. 'Now get yourself back on the road,' Señor Buho commanded. 'You nearly gave me a heart attack. We have no time to waste – I told you this part of the journey would be dangerous. You really must be more careful.'

Poohka had not long regained consciousness, and the pain was so intense. He was also feeling very, very bruised, but he knew he had to carry on with the rest of the journey, and he could only do it with Señor Buho's help. 'Why is Señor Buho being so cruel to me?' Poohka wondered.

It took what seemed like forever, but Poohka eventually climbed his way up the rocks, one paw at a time, with his broken leg still dangling, getting in the way.

Señor Buho was frantically flying back and forth over the road. 'I've checked for cars, and the road is clear!' Señor Buho circled above Poohka. 'Now for goodness' sake, hurry up and get around this dangerous corner as fast as you can.'

Poohka did the best he could, but he looked down at his broken leg and he saw a new open wound – with a bone protruding! Poohka's stomach turned, but he looked away. He knew he needed help more than ever, but for now he had to continue on three legs.

'Keep looking ahead,' he told himself, for every time he looked at the damaged leg a wave of nausea would hit him. With determination he picked up speed on his other three legs and tried to blank out the pain.

As they journeyed onwards, Señor Buho stayed closer. 'You are doing well, lad,' Señor Buho called out to Poohka. Poohka looked up in surprise – this was the first time he had ever given him any encouragement. 'Only ten more kilometres to go,' added the owl.

Poohka's spirits lifted, and he walked on three legs with even more purpose. The hilly terrain had now flattened out and, although still difficult, it was certainly much easier than before.

Every now and then, Poohka thought of Pequita, and his heart ached. He would so dearly have liked to have stayed with her. Now all he had was the memory of her which he would cherish forever. 'Oh, Pequita I will miss you!' He knew he'd probably never get to see her again but his only chance was to survive this journey. So the thought of Pequita, sad as it was, gave him the extra courage he needed to carry on despite the pain.

Then, in the early hours of the morning of the 22nd September 2006, Poohka rounded a corner and found himself at the barriers to the northern side of Sotogrande. He was home!

Chapter 15 - Will Poohka make it?

Just one thing stood in the way of Poohka's homecoming. Before he could reach the barriers he had to cross a giant road where cars whizzed left and right without a second's gap between them.

Poohka looked up at Señor Buho. But the owl had no answers. 'Well, I can fly over, of course,' said Señor Buho. 'You will have to run across.'

Poohka stared at the road. There were three lanes on this side, and another three on the other. There was just no way he'd be able to cross it and survive. The cars flashed past so fast they were blurry.

'Come on, Poohka,' said Señor Buho. 'You are nearly home!'

It was true – he was nearly home. But to Poohka, it still felt like he was a million miles away. Perhaps it would be better to go back to Pequita than to try to cross this road and get flattened. But then Poohka glanced down at his broken leg and sickness bubbled in his stomach. He had to get to Sotogrande for help.

He studied the road carefully while Señor Buho circled above. It seemed that every couple of minutes there was a tiny lull in the traffic on this side – and then two minutes later, a lull on the other.

'Come on, Poohka!' Señor Buho called out.

'Wait, I'm thinking!' Poohka replied. He focused back on the road. Yes, he was sure there was a gap in the traffic every so often – perhaps caused by traffic lights further away. The lull was only a few seconds – but perhaps it was enough time for him to get to the centre of the road and wait there for the lull on the other side, before finally finishing the crossing.

Poohka took a deep breath. This was very dangerous. After all

he'd been through, he knew it should seem simple. But to Poohka, even though he was so close to home, he felt like his biggest test was yet to come.

The gap was almost there. It was now or never.

Poohka ignored the pain in his broken leg and as a red car flew past he scampered into the road. The tarmac was hot under his feet and the noise of cars frightening, but he kept going.

'You can do it!' Poohka heard Señor Buho cry.

Poohka was almost at the centre, and then he felt gravel underfoot. He'd made it halfway! Poohka swung back around and saw the cars rushing along the road behind him. A warm wave of achievement flooded through him. But it wasn't over yet. He focused again on the traffic ahead. He felt a lump in his throat. The gap here was even shorter. Would it be enough time to get over?

Poohka didn't have any more time to think. The gap had arrived.

He rushed out, quite used to the hot tarmac by now and the smell of rubber that steamed up from the road. But as he scampered over, he heard the roar of an engine getting closer. 'Not yet!' he thought. 'The cars shouldn't be coming yet!'

But one car was. Poohka looked to his side and saw the grill of a huge white truck rushing up the road towards him. Fear told him to freeze, but he knew he had to keep going, and not give in to his terror. He swung back around and ran as fast as his three legs could take him, squeezing his eyes shut as he went. All he could do was hope.

'Poohka, are you OK?' said a gentle voice in his ear.

'Senor Buho! Did I make it?' Poohka asked, his eyes still squeezed shut.

'You did. You were incredible!' said the wise old owl.

Poohka opened one eye, and then the other. Sure enough, he was safely on the other side of the road – the Sotogrande side!

'It was a close call when that truck came along too fast – I thought you were a goner,' Señor Buho told Poohka. 'But I've never seen you move so quickly.'

Poohka felt a moment of complete happiness. He was nearly home. He picked himself up with renewed energy. 'Let's go!' he said to Señor Buho. 'Not far now!'

Poohka hobbled quietly past the security man sitting in the hut by the barriers. The cat could see the man watching the security screen in front of him, oblivious to Poohka passing by on the grass verge into the Sotogrande Estate.

Poohka carried on the road, heading to the roundabout in the direction of Almenara Golf Club.

'Poohka,' called Señor Buho, 'soon I will have to leave you. I need to return to my family before day breaks. I will see you as far as the roundabout ahead, then all you will have to do is turn left and just carry on. It is much safer here, and there are many trees and bushes for you to use as shelter during daylight hours,' Señor Buho explained.

As they reached the roundabout, Señor Buho landed close to Poohka and in his gruff voice said, 'It has been nice getting to know you, Poohka. If I have seemed uncaring and maybe even rude or abrupt at times, it has all been intended for your own interest. Sometimes you have to be cruel to be kind.'

Poohka nodded. He thought he understood what Señor Buho was saying. However cruel the wise owl had been, without his help, Poohka would have never made it home.

'Now you are on your own, but I suggest you have a rest before you walk the remainder of your journey. Good luck. I wish you a good life back in Sotogrande. Adios, young lad. Take care.' And with that, Señor Buho took flight and was gone.

'Thank you, Señor Buho, thank you for everything...' Poohka called after him, but once again Poohka did not have a chance to say all the things he wanted to say to thank Señor Buho properly.

With the glimmer of early morning light, Poohka could just about make out Señor Buho circling high in the sky as though saying one last final farewell.

Poohka chose a large bush to settle under. After his last battle with the road he was exhausted, and although he was close to home, he wanted to clean his nasty wound and prepare himself for the last part of his journey. He would be there by nightfall. But now he desperately needed to rest.

Poohka spent time cleaning his wound, but his stomach turned as he did so. The leg was now so badly damaged it was unrecognisable, and he desperately hoped someone would help him and it could be mended. Most of all he wanted the pain to disappear once and for all.

Poohka closed his eyes and slept fitfully. Eventually tiredness overwhelmed him and he fell into a deep, dreamless sleep.

Poohka woke with a start. A sprinkler system had started to water the area where he was hiding. Although his heart was pounding it came as a welcome surprise – he was able to quench his thirst before completing the last part of his journey.

Realising that the heat of the day had passed and early evening was setting in, Poohka set off again. Compared to all the previous days, this was going to be easy.

Now he could see the rubbish skips in the external parking area of the estate. He had come a long way since that fateful day chasing prawns. He would never make such a mistake again, of that he was absolutely positive. So, with his head held high, he hobbled his way through the security check point. Poohka saw it was Bella's shift, and that she was busy sorting out paperwork into each of the mail drops. She did not notice Poohka making his way under the barriers.

Poohka was in search of just one thing: 3jabs. He ignored his throbbing leg and hobbled towards the workers' hut.

'Hey, mate, where've you been?!' exclaimed 3jabs as Poohka turned the corner into the workers' area. 3jabs rushed over to his friend, but stopped dead in his tracks when he saw Poohka's front leg. 'That's not looking good. You need help, mate. But, boy, am I glad to see you. We all thought you were a goner! Have you got lots to tell us? First we need to get you fixed! Where have you been? You look terrible! Have you eaten?' 3jabs continued talking without taking a breath.

He brought over some food. 'Eat plenty – they haven't long put the food down, but this means we aren't likely to see anyone who could help you until tomorrow.' 3jabs looked again at Poohka's leg. 'But, mate, I think you need to see someone now!'

Poohka picked at the crunchy food. He did not have much of an appetite with all the emotions going on inside him. Poohka was happy beyond words to be home, but he still had one very grave problem: his mangled, broken leg.

'3jabs, I have so much to tell you, but first I need help. Do you think you could find Greta, Robert, Alex or Annabel – oh, just anyone who will help me?'

'Stay right where you are. I'll go and get someone for you. Hang in there, mate. We'll get you sorted.' 3jabs shot off in the direction of Annabel and Alex's apartment building.

3jabs was gone for a few minutes, and in that time several feral cats began crowding around Poohka. They fired hundreds of questions at him, but all Poohka wanted was help. He collapsed by the food containers – his energy had almost run out. Where had 3jabs got to?

Just as Poohka was about to close his eyes, 3jabs came rushing up to him, barging his way past the gathering of cats.

'Stop crowding Poohka – move out of the way. He needs help.

Stop asking him so many questions, we will all find out what happened to him in time.'

3jabs moved closer to his friend. 'I tried to get someone's help, but they didn't notice me – I'm just another cat, after all. But I have an idea. Mate, can you manage to lift yourself up, then walk just a little more? If we position ourselves at the rear of Alex and Annabel's apartment, just to the side of Greta and Robert's, then we can all make a lot of noise, and they might see how badly your leg is broken. Then help will be at hand. It's our best chance.'

Poohka summoned his last reserves of energy and very slowly lifted his weary body. He wobbled on his three legs, trying desperately to keep his balance. 3jabs and the other cats gave him encouragement. They all made their way around to the back of the apartment block, Poohka limping along at a snail's pace. By the time they arrived in position the sun was setting. Being the last week in September there were very few people around. Most of the holiday makers had left and the private estate was once again quiet and peaceful.

The cats began to meow, gently at first, but then louder and louder. But there were no lights on in Alex and Annabel's apartment, nor in Greta and Robert's. 3jabs explained to Poohka that he'd seen their Land Rover leave, but it hadn't returned.

Luck just wasn't on Poohka's side. With a heavy heart, he realised he would have to wait until morning.

As the cats sat, hoping, waiting, Poohka began to tell his story. He was weary, but he wanted to explain where he'd been. His friends sat aghast as they heard what had happened to their friend. Poohka was truly lucky to be alive, even if he had sustained such bad injuries.

'Oh, mate, you have had a terrible time,' said 3jabs. 'But tell me – what was Pequita like? Was she REALLY beautiful? Do you think she is my type?' Poohka laughed – as always 3jabs liked to talk and attract the ladies!

As the night wore on, eventually it was just Poohka and 3jabs who remained in the apartment block area. They knew they would have to wait until dawn to try to get help.

Just before 3jabs closed his eyes to sleep, he turned to Poohka. 'It's great to have you back, Poohka, I missed you, mate. I thought something really terrible had happened to you.'

In a weak voice Poohka softly replied, 'Thank you, 3jabs. It is good to be back with all of my friends again.'

Chapter 16 - Landing on my feet

As dawn broke, Poohka and 3jabs meowed constantly at the apartments, hoping that someone would hear and come to help.

A door suddenly opened on the terrace above, and to Poohka's relief, Annabel's head popped out.

'Oh, Poohka!' Annabel cried. 'Thank goodness you are still alive and you have come back to us. But what's happened to your leg?'

Poohka smiled at 3jabs as they heard Annabel run inside and call to Alex, 'Quickly, Alex, Poohka is back, but he's badly injured. We must get him to the vet straightaway.'

Moments later, Annabel ran out with the pet carrier to the back of the block. At the sight of Annabel, Poohka tried to hobble towards her.

'Oh, Poohka, you poor thing!' Annabel cried.

Poohka purred with delight at seeing Annabel and the relief of knowing that, at last, everything would be all right.

Alex already had the Land Rover running and once Poohka was safely aboard, they drove straight to the vet's, calling on the way to let them know they were bringing in an injured cat.

The road to the vet's surgery had not improved since 3jabs's visit – in fact it was even worse than 3jabs had described. The bumpy ride made Poohka meow in pain.

'Don't worry, Poohka,' said Alex, 'we will have you at the vet's in no time.'

When they arrived, Antonio greeted them at the door. 'Bring Poohka straight into the surgery, please.'

Very gently, Annabel lifted Poohka out of the carrier, and looked into Poohka's pleading eyes. 'Don't worry, Poohka, we'll get you sorted out. You're going to be all right.'

'This isn't looking good,' Antonio said after taking a closer look at Poohka's leg. 'I can possibly fix it, but the cat will no longer be able to survive in the wild. It's kinder to put him down.'

Poohka winced at the thought. After all he'd been through – they were going to put him down?

But Alex was shaking his head. 'You must do whatever you can to save Poohka. He will not return to the wild, I promise you. If Annabel agrees we will look after him ourselves.'

Annabel nodded, and Poohka's heart leapt – he was going to survive, and live with Alex and Annabel!

Annabel and Alex looked at each other across the table and said in unison, 'Poohka must be saved.'

Antonio wasted no time after that. He collected a syringe and inserted a strong antibiotic into Poohka. Alex and Annabel said farewell to Poohka and left the surgery leaving Antonio to begin cleaning the wound. Poohka stayed perfectly still while Antonio took a closer look at his badly damaged leg. The pain was immense and occasionally he let out an agonising meow, but in his heart he was so grateful and relieved that someone was going to save him.

When Poohka woke up from his operation he felt groggy and strange. He looked down to see his leg but it wasn't there anymore! It had been amputated!

Poohka felt sick to his stomach. He'd lost his leg! How on earth would he survive like this? He'd never manage on the streets with only three legs. What would he do?

Then he remembered Alex and Annabel's promise. He wouldn't have to survive in the wild any more. He was to be a house cat! It was the cosy life of luxury for him from now on. So if there was ever a good time to lose a leg, I guess this was it.

Pookha was certainly grateful that the awful pain had gone. But the idea of the rest of his life with only three legs was something that was going to take some getting used to. 'Still, I guess I'm just lucky to be alive at all,' he thought, 'after all I've been through.'

Poohka remained at the vet's hospital for three weeks. In that time he didn't see Annabel and Alex once, which worried Poohka. Were they going to take him home and look after him? Or had they changed their minds? Each day he got a little stronger, but he also became more convinced that Annabel and Alex weren't going to look after him after all. By the third week, Poohka was certain he had been abandoned. The prospect of trying to survive in the wild with only three legs was something too awful to consider.

'What is to become of me?' Poohka asked himself time after time.

It was exactly twenty-one days after his operation when Poohka recognised the sound of Alex and Annabel's voices. His heart skipped a beat. They had come back for him!

He anxiously lifted himself up and slowly balanced himself on his three legs.

'Poohka, how good to see you.' Annabel looked at him lovingly. 'I am sorry we were so long but we had to take a trip to England, and we knew Antonio would take good care of you here. We telephoned every day to check how you were doing. But now we have come to take you home.' She stroked his head and rubbed his chin as she spoke.

Poohka purred as if he had never purred before. If he'd been able to skip around he would have! 'I am going home!' thought Poohka as he let out another contented meow.

Alex was turning the car around when Annabel emerged with the pet carrier containing one very contented cat. As they drove along, Annabel asked, 'How do you think Poppins and Cosmos will be when they see our new member of the family? Do you think Poppins will be jealous of another cat coming into her home?'

'Very likely,' replied Alex, 'but I am sure Cosmos will be pleased to have some male support.'

Poohka's heart jumped a beat. 'I am going to be part of a family – in a proper home. How COOL is that?' he thought to himself. 'First, I must win over Poppins, then hopefully she will learn to love me. And Cosmos may be able to teach me a few things expected of family cats.' Excited thoughts whizzed through Poohka's mind.

Poohka arrived at the apartment feeling as if he was the most fortunate cat in the world.

'I will put Poohka in the guest bedroom so he can adapt to living indoors, and we will gradually introduce him to Poppins and Cosmos in a couple of days,' Annabel decided.

Poppins and Cosmos soon took to Poohka once he had settled in. And Poohka quickly adapted to his three legs. He found that by placing the front leg more centrally as he walked he was able to do most of the things he did before.

It was not long before Poohka was fully recovered from the operation, enjoying life and tearing around the place. Cosmos was a wise old cat and he gave Poohka lots of advice – some of it Poohka listened to, and some he did not. Poohka liked to run wild at great speed around the apartment. Cosmos soon pointed out, 'Poohka, the reason you are no good at going round corners is because you are going far too fast. Too much acceleration! I know in your heart you may think you are an Aston Martin, but in reality, Poohka, you are a Reliant Robin. Now please behave as one!'

But this remark did not deter Poohka. He could run, pain free, and he wasn't going to stop going as fast as he could. After his epic and painful journey to get home, he felt like a sports car – not a three-wheeler!

Poohka enjoyed spending his days luxuriating on the terrace, napping for many happy hours on the large, circular revolving seat and sharing it with both Poppins and Cosmos. Most days, Poohka sat for long periods on the wall of the terrace, looking down and chatting to his old chums below in the gardens of the estate. He missed 3jabs and his other friends, but they knew he wasn't able to join them and they were happy that at least he was alive and enjoying a good life with only three legs.

And at night, when Poohka heard the hoot of an owl, he would look up and think of Señor Buho, Señor Arbol and all the animals who helped him on his journey, and think about how lucky he was to have received such kindness.

One afternoon, two years later, a beautiful part-Siamese cat turned up in Sotogrande. It was Pequita!

Poohka was half-asleep when 3jabs escorted Pequita onto the grass in front of the terrace. But even through one tired eye and after two years apart, Poohka recognized immediately who it was.

'Pequita!' he cried. 'You came!'

'Did you think I'd forgotten you, sweet Poohka?' she purred. 'I've thought of you every day for the last two years but you've been a little hard to find...'

Pequita was just as lovely as he remembered her and he was overjoyed to see her. They soon got talking about the last two years, catching up on all they had missed. Pequita was sad Poohka had lost the leg and that she couldn't get closer to him in his new home. But it was enough to have found him again.

From then on, Pequita visited every day, standing at the base of the terrace and looking up longingly at Poohka, talking and laughing. Poohka was happy, knowing that Pequita had a little hut below the terrace where she slept in comfort, and they could spend their days together, just as they had said they would.

Each evening, before closing his eyes to go to sleep, Poohka always said to Poppins and Cosmos: 'You know, I am the luckiest cat in the world. I may only have three legs, but I have certainly landed on my feet!'

THE END

Adelaide Godwin

Adelaide was educated at an Ursuline convent in a remote Belgian village before attending Winkfield Place Finishing School, famous as Constance Spry's school. There she achieved a Cordon Bleu Diploma and went on to work for Prue Leith in London and as chef at the Little London Restaurant in Chichester.

Adelaide then joined British Airways and took to the skies, working as Cabin Crew for fifteen years and travelling the world extensively.

Adelaide has also worked in the television and film industry doing small acting roles, as well as some photographic and voiceover work.

She now divides her time between homes in the UK and southern Spain where she cares for animals, writes, paints and enjoys the Mediterranean sunshine.

Acknowledgements

To my helpers: Mike, Frankie, Leila, Zoe, Henry, Goisa, Richard, Lauren, Olivia, Catherine, Alice and Carmen.

To my family and friends for their love and support.

Of course the biggest thank you goes to Poohka himself, who has given us so much joy and love. Without Poohka, this book would not have been possible.

In loving memory of my dear father; also Poppins, Cosmos and 3jabs, and all the other animals who have touched my life.

Also in memory of dear Lynette and Rachel.